DEVIL'S BRIDE

Rachelle Edwards

A FAWCETT CREST BOOK

Fawcett Publications, Inc., Greenwich, Connecticut

DEVIL'S BRIDE

THIS BOOK CONTAINS THE COMPLETE TEXT OF THE
ORIGINAL HARDCOVER EDITION.

A Fawcett Crest Book reprinted by arrangement with Robert
Hale & Company

ISBN 0-449-23176-3

Printed in the United States of America

10   9   8   7   6   5   4   3   2   1

"Now please to get dressed, Miss Stanford."

She looked up at duke sharply. "Why?"

"We are leaving."

His tone denoted an endless patience that was deceiving, and Auriol, at such a peremptory order, stiffened.

"I have no intention of leaving here tonight, and certainly not with you."

His eyes burned into her. "You will, Miss Stanford, you most certainly will even if I have to carry you out on my back dressed just as you are now, which will give the landlord and his lackeys some amusement."

Auriol knew it was no idle threat. Moreover he would enjoy doing so and her eyes swam with the tears she was determined not to shed in his presence.

"You are a fiend," she cried. "My stepfather must have been mad to accept you."

"Not mad, Miss Stanford," he answered mildly, "simply anxious for a step up the social ladder. 'Tis a natural aspiration."

"Did he send you after me?"

"No, it was my own idea entirely. I had no fancy to have it known my betrothed had eloped with another man."

DEVIL'S BRIDE

Part One

Now hatred is by far the longest pleasure
Men love in haste but they detest at leisure

I

The library door closed with a bang that resounded around the cavernous hall of number nineteen Mount Street in the heart of Mayfair.

Auriol Stanford paused outside the library. Her hands tightened around her riding whip as she stared furiously into space. After a moment or two she took a deep breath and then, still wearing her tailored riding habit, she stormed up the stairs. A small spaniel frisked at her heels, quite unconcerned about her mistress's fury, which, anyway, was never directed towards her. Auriol carried the riding whip in both her hands and it looked as if she were ready to lash out with it at any moment, as she had been known to do on occasions, to those unfortunate enough to cause her displeasure.

A footman stood as immobile as a statue outside the drawing room but before he could spring to open the doors for her, Auriol had done it for herself, flinging them back abruptly. At the suddenness of her entry the languid figure lying on a day bed sat up, startled by the intrusion. The footman closed the doors in a way far more gentle than the one in which they had been thrust open as the young woman marched purposefully across the room. The recumbent figure raised itself still further. She smiled uncertainly and then looked fearful at the expression she saw on the young girl's face.

"Auriol," her mother sighed, "you look quite put out. What is amiss, dear?"

"Need you ask?"

At last she gave way to the fury that was tearing away at her and she threw down the riding whip which the spaniel seized and proceeded to chew. Auriol ignored her pet and impatiently pulled off her plumed riding hat, leaving her hair in some disarray. She wore it unpowdered and as she stood before her mother, her eyes flashing like a pair of emeralds, the sun streamed through the window lighting her hair with fire.

"I have just had an interview with Mr Ardmore. A most surprising interview, I must declare. No doubt you already know what it is about, Mama."

The Ladies' Magazine which Mrs Ardmore had been reading slipped from her lap on to the floor. "Well, my dear," she said timidly, "has he not told you the wonderful news?"

"Wonderful news! Oh, Mama!" She turned away so that her mother should not see the tears of frustration and anger that sprang to her eyes. And then, a moment later, she turned round, composed again. "I refuse. I absolutely refuse to marry that awful man. There is no question of it! You may as well be warned."

Her mother shrank back into the cushions. "Auriol, it is the Duke of Hampden who wishes to marry you."

"So Mr Ardmore informed me, but the Duke has said nothing of it to me even though the opportunity has arisen at least four times in the last se'nnight."

The woman's turbanned head shook slowly. "It would have been entirely improper of him to do so until he had obtained the proper permission from your step-father."

"Faddle. He should have addressed me first. This is the way of it today. Times have changed since your youth, Mama."

"He called to see your step-father this afternoon whilst you were out riding. He was not to know your feelings in this matter." She gave a timid little laugh. "He is not perhaps as modern as you, dear."

"No one deemed it important to discover my feelings. 'Tis only *my* future in question, and yet already it is all agreed. The trustees of Father's estate agree too. Oh, it is too bad!"

"You will be a duchess," her mother said coaxingly, knowing her daughter's pride and love of finery.

"But I don't want to be a duchess if he is to be my duke." Auriol's mother winced. "I abhor that man, Mama. Did you know that? I declare I never knew how much until this piece of impudence today. He has never paid court to me as others have done before offering for me. How dare he be so presumptuous?"

"Presumptuous, my dear?" asked her mother in

some bewilderment. "He is the only man who has acted with propriety."

Suddenly all Auriol's anger drained from her. Her chin trembled and tears misted her eyes, and she sank down on to the end of the day bed, bursting into tears.

"I can't bear the thought of it, Mama."

She sobbed heartbrokenly into her hands. Her mother, accustomed more to Auriol's tantrums rather than her tears, could do no more than pat her daughter's hand and murmur, "Now, now, my dear, you must see that this marriage will bring you great prestige." Auriol only shook her head and cried the harder. "You haven't the ability to decide such matters for yourself. Parents are far wiser in such matters than children."

"I am not a child, Mama," Auriol argued, sniffing loudly into her handkerchief. "I'd as lief marry any man in London as the Duke of Hampden."

"I cannot conceive why you should dislike him so, Auriol. He is a very handsome man to be sure."

"He is old."

"No more than *thirty*," Mrs Ardmore laughed shakily. "Why, I am more than that, and I am not *old*."

Auriol dried her tears and smiled tremulously at her mother. Relieved to some extent Isabella Ardmore sank back into the cushions once again.

"Mama, I want to marry Mr Dainton. Surely you and Mr Ardmore were aware of my wishes in this respect."

Mrs Ardmore's face froze momentaritly and then she smiled. "Certainly we were aware you harboured a penchant for this young man, and indeed he is a very pleasant and presentable fellow, but my dear, marriages even today are not made purely on the basis of fondness and he is a penniless nobody."

Auriol, having recovered from one of her rare excursions into tears, was becoming angry again. "The Duke is penniless also. There is no secret about that."

"He is a duke." Mrs Ardmore became alert again having found the correct ammunition with which to fight her battle. "His ancestors go back as far as Richard Coeur de Lion."

"I love Mr Dainton, Mama," Auriol insisted.

"Oh, faddle, Auriol. Now I am becoming impatient with you. Love indeed. That is of no account."

Auriol looked at her mother with eyes that had reduced many a proud buck into a lovelorn swain. "Can you not persuade Mr Ardmore to change his mind? If I cannot marry Mr Dainton I shall break my heart."

Mrs Ardmore began to feel uncomfortable beneath such an appealing look, but with rare purpose she steeled herself against it.

"It is inconceivable for a girl of your fortune to marry beneath the rank of earl. This offer is far better than we could have hoped for, so you'd best make the most of it, for your step-father will not change his mind. Nor should he. The agreement is made." She could no longer meet her daughter's eyes and see them filled with such anguish. "Why on earth couldn't you fall in love with him, if, indeed, *love* is so important to you? From what I hear and see every other young filly has been smitten by him."

"That may well be, Mama, but his Grace, the Duke of Hampden, has eyes for only one lady, if indeed she can be called that," Auriol said bitterly. Unconsciously she was tearing her delicate cambric handkerchief to pieces as she spoke.

Her mother looked even more uncomfortable. "And who, may I ask, may that be?"

"You know as well as everyone else in London— Madame Gillray. A widow, indeed," she scoffed. "As if anyone has ever known *Monsieur Gillray*. She is nothing more than a French lightskirt!"

"Auriol, your language!"

"He'll use my inheritance to keep her in that palace he bought her in Portman Square," she went on heatedly, ignoring her mother's outrage.

"That need not concern *you*. Don't be so silly, Auriol. Even at your age you must know that most men have their . . . diversions. You will be his wife. It need not concern you for one moment."

"I will not marry a man who loves another."

"It is not many weeks since Mr Dainton fancied himself in love with Miss Helena Brittain."

"That was a passing fancy."

"He offered for her and was turned down. That does not seem like a passing fancy to me, and, Auriol, whilst we are on the subject, I must mention that Mr Dainton seems to have a strange habit of falling in love with girls who have a very substantial portion."

"Mr Dainton is *not* a fortune hunter. He loves me, and," she added softly, "I love him."

"Love! Love! Love! La! What nonsense you talk, Auriol. I do declare you will not find a man of any worth who does not entertain amusements outside his home. You will marry the Duke and then you may find love where you will, if you must."

Auriol jumped to her feet. "The thought of it appals me. I cannot be as the Duchess of Devonshire, great lady that she is, to have the Duke's *chère amie* under her roof as her bosom friend."

"The Duchess has her own interests. As I tell you, once you are wed you may do as you please."

Auriol put her hands to her lips and closed her eyes. "Oh, Crispin, Crispin, what am I to do?"

"You will think better of it in an hour or two," her mother said kindly, "when you have had time to reflect on the advantages of such a match, and there are many.

"This has been something of a shock—to both of us," she added, sinking further back into the cushions.

Auriol turned on her then. "You married for love, Mama. You married Papa because you loved him. Do you not remember that?"

"Yes," she answered wearily, "I remember it all too well, and it was a disastrous marriage. I was left a widow with a small child before I was twenty years old. Only Lady Luck ensured he did not leave us penniless when he died. He had not enough time to gamble away his fortune. Let me tell you now, Auriol, there is no advantage in marrying for love."

"You would not have had him otherwise. When you speak of him there is a certain nuance in your voice. I recognise it, Mama."

Isabella Ardmore's eyes softened at the memory of the moment and then her expression hardened again. "Nor would I wish such an improvident man for my daughter."

"Mr Dainton is of a sober disposition but the Duke of Hampden is a gambler as well as a rake."

Mrs Ardmore waved her hand in the air. "The Duke is of quite a different stamp to your father; he is no fool. If I were a little younger I believe I could be a little in love with him myself."

"Mama!" her daughter cried impatiently.

Isabella Ardmore laughed in embarrassment. "I chose carefully the second time. Mr Ardmore is neither a gambler nor a rake, Auriol."

Auriol drew in a sharp breath at the mention of her step-father. "No, he is not that. He is a mean and sanctimonious toady."

Her mother gasped in shock and surprise. Auriol was well known to be plain spoken but she had never before spoken with such disrespect.

"I will not have you speak of your step-father thus. Apologise for that remark, Auriol, or I'll box your ears."

Auriol bit her lip. "I apologise to you, Mama, but I cannot apologise for speaking the truth, and if you will only admit it to yourself you know I am right. You have, this past ten years, taken to your couch rather than stand up to him. Well, I do not wish for such a fate and I am not yet beaten. He gained a rich wife by marrying you, but he shall not climb the ladder of Society on my back by marrying me to that hellrake!"

So saying, she turned on her heel and rushed from the room, her mother's cries echoing in her ears. She ran unseeing because of her tears and when she reached the sanctuary of her room she flung herself on her bed, sobbing hysterically with her face buried in the counterpane.

In the drawing room Isabella Ardmore stumbled to

her feet and called for a footman to fetch her maid. The woman arrived moments later to find her mistress half fainting on the couch.

"My vinaigrette!" she gasped. "Oh, the ungrateful wretch. To think . . . I had hoped for a brilliant match for my girl all these years . . . and now . . . The ingratitude is not to be borne!"

II

Auriol lay on her bed staring up at the pink damask tester. All passion was spent now; she had no more tears to shed. Now she was left with the firm resolution to die rather than to marry the Duke of Hampden. Suki, the spaniel, lay asleep curled up beside her mistress on the bed and unthinkingly Auriol stroked her silky fur.

When her maid came into the room some time later Auriol slipped off the bed and attempted to make some appearance of normality.

Hannah bobbed a curtsey. "Your riding clothes are all crushed, ma'am," she said, amazed to see her mistress recumbent in her outdoor clothes.

"It doesn't matter," came the dull answer.

She allowed Hannah to help her out of her clothes and when she was wrapped in a satinet gown she sank down wearily at the dressing table.

"The green watered silk, ma'am?" Hannah asked perfunctorily as she took out the gown. "And how will you have your hair? Six feathers will be sufficient, I think."

Auriol stared at her pale, tear-stained face in the looking glass. A pair of red rimmed eyes looked back at her. Lady Hartington's rout. In the tumult of the afternoon she had forgotten all about it. She buried her face in her hands at the reminder of the evening's engagements. Hampden was certain to be there.

No. She could not face him now; to see him gloat, watch him being congratulated. It was her fortune he wanted; there was no doubt about that. He had won the most eligible heiress of the Season without presenting so much as a posy of flowers or one flattering word.

Auriol fought the insane desire to laugh. Everyone would think her mad to prefer Crispin Dainton, the impoverished son a country parson, when a duke was making an offer. But even if she were not in love with another, the Duke of Hampden was the last man on earth she would want to marry. She abhorred his arrogance, and there was something about his manner, exemplary as it was, that frightened her.

Hannah placed the patch box on the dressing table and then began to remove the pins from Auriol's bronze curls. Auriol put her hand out to stay her.

"This will not be necessary. I shall not be going out this evening. Be so kind as to inform my step-father that I am unwell and I am going to bed."

Hannah just looked at her, for she had never yet known Miss Stanford to miss an important social occasion. "You do look pale, ma'am," she murmured a moment later.

"Yes, yes I know that. Don't just stand there staring at me. Do as you are told."

Hannah now hastened to obey and then when she reached the door she asked timidly, "Shall I have the physician summoned, ma'am?"

"No! I need only rest . . . and peace."

"Shall I fetch you some broth then when I return. If you are to miss your dinner you must eat something."

Ashamed of her hasty tongue she nodded. "Thank you, Hannah, I shall probably appreciate that."

When the girl returned some time later with the broth she found her mistress pacing the room, wringing her hands together in anguish.

"Have they gone yet, Hannah?" she asked anxiously. "Mr and Mrs Ardmore."

"Yes, ma'am; not five minutes ago."

Auriol let out a sigh of relief. She had some respite now; not long but better than nothing. She must think of some way out of this ghastly situation before morning. There was little time to be lost.

"Come and eat your broth, ma'am, before it gets cold," Hannah urged.

But Auriol was not listening. "I cannot face this alone," she cried. "I just don't know what to do!"

She hurried across to her writing desk and began to pull out sheets of paper. "Hannah, can I trust you on a mission of the utmost urgency and complete secrecy?"

The girl looked bewildered but nevertheless nodded her head. "Yes, ma'am. You know I'd do anything I can to help you. You only need ask it of me."

Auriol smiled. "I am indeed fortunate in having

you serve me, Hannah. I promise you will not lose by your fidelity to me.

"It is imperative that you deliver this message to Mr Dainton without anyone seeing you, and with no delay. Is that understood?"

The girl nodded. "Yes, ma'am, I quite understand. You may rely upon me."

"You must hurry to his lodgings or you will miss him. I'm afraid I cannot risk sending a groom to escort you. The less people who know about this the better it will be, but it is not far to Mr Dainton's lodgings. Tell no one where you are bound. This must not be intercepted. It is for Mr Dainton's eyes only."

The girl nodded again, her eyes wide with wonder as Auriol picked up the quill and began to scratch across the page as quickly as she could.

III

The street in which stood Lady Hartington's town house was crammed with horsedrawn carriages. The barouche conveying Mr and Mrs Septimus Ardmore came to a halt, waiting its turn to disgorge its passengers in front of the pillared portico of the Hartington mansion which was ablaze with lights.

Septimus Ardmore put his head out of the window for a moment and then sank back into the cushions to await their arrival. His wife stared ahead unseeingly, not caring if they never reached their destination. She had an abominable headache and wished her husband had not insisted that they attend Lady Hartington's rout; but Lady Hartington was one of the leaders of the beau monde and an invitation to one of her assemblies was one that Septimus Ardmore would not miss.

"Really, my dear," he said mildly as the carriage moved forward a few paces, "I wish Auriol could have seen fit to attend this evening. It's too bad of her."

"She has not taken the news well," she ventured, broaching the subject for the first time.

A dull red suffused his already florid cheeks. "She was most insolent to me, Isabella," he said severely. "I was only restrained from inflicting on her the most severe punishment by recalling this was such a shock to her as it was to us."

"You are so good, Septimus. She does not deserve your consideration of her. She should be eternally grateful to you for being such a good father."

He looked gratified now. "She will, in due course, learn how much she owes to me, and I am certain she will soon become resigned to her coming marriage. You know, my dear, your daughter protests for no better reason than to thwart me. It has been so since the day you and I were wed."

His wife looked doubtful. "That may well be so, dear, and you know it has always grieved me most sorely, for you are always so good, but she was very adamant this time."

Her husband looked outraged again. "She has no right to be. Can she not trust me to arrange her affairs satisfactorily? Have I not always done so?"

"Oh yes, indeed, dear."

Septimus Ardmore was once more mollified. "Do you not realise, Isabella, that as well as being the greatest honour for your daughter, when she is the Duchess of Hampden there will be no doors closed to us?" He rubbed his hands together in anticipation, forgetting his earlier ire. "No credit refused."

His wife chuckled, forgetting too her earlier unease.

"I can hardly wait to inform Dorothea Makepeace. La! When I think of all that posturing just because her daughter married a viscount last Season!"

"Your daughter, Madam, proud creature that she is, will soon come to appreciate the advantages of marrying a man of high rank; the highest except for a prince, and handsome as she is, we cannot really expect *that*."

"Haven't I always suffered slights because of my lack of title?"

"But you have so much more to make up for it, my dear."

Septimus beamed, lost in anticipation of his future. "His Grace is the most generous of men, Isabella. He has promised me a pair of greys from his own stables. Two of the most splendid creatures you ever did see. And we shall spend summers at Hampden Towers; think of that. Invitations, I recall, were always hard come by in the past when the last Duchess was alive."

"Oh, 'twill be splendid. My daughter, a duchess!" Her delight faded as suddenly as it had come. "But Septimus, she was so distraught. Do you think she will really become reconciled to it?"

"Naturally," he answered in a stiff manner. "The betrothal was arranged for her benefit, not mine."

"She worries me so, Septimus. Her will is so strong when she has her mind made up. She is so very like her father and he was such a hothead."

Septimus Ardmore's lips drew into a thin line of disapproval. "Yes, so I believe, which makes her marriage to Hampden doubly opportune. The girl is wealthy and needs someone like myself to ensure she does not squander it. I have had responsibility for it for too long with no thanks for my pains, for as you know, your daughter has been a difficult child to discipline. The Duke is a man who will know how to tame a firebrand," he added grimly.

His wife looked at him in alarm but at that moment the carriage jerked forward to stop outside Hartington House, and a footman was lowering the steps. Mrs Ardmore had no choice but to step down and force a smile to her lips.

IV

Auriol just could not keep still. Endlessly she paced the floor. She had been seated for a while but she had now resumed her restless pacing, for no magazine or book could command her attention tonight. The carriage clock on the mantelshelf struck the hour and the candles were burned low in their sockets. Hannah had been gone but a short while and yet it seemed an age.

At last, when the door opened, Auriol was so startled that she cried out, and then recovering herself she darted forward to greet her maid.

"Did you discover him at home?"

"Yes, ma'am," the girl answered breathlessly. "Mr Dainton was just about to go out when I arrived so I was not a moment too soon!"

"And his reply?"

"Mr Dainton was very disturbed by your letter,

ma'am, and he insisted on coming right back with me."

Auriol's hands flew to her cheeks. "Crispin here!" she gasped. "Where is he? Not in the drawing room surely?"

Hannah smiled. "I thought it best to bring him round the back. I hope I did right, ma'am. He's waiting downstairs, in the butler's pantry." She lowered her eyes in embarrassment. "Dennison's drunk, ma'am, and with one of the parlour maids, so I reckoned it would be safe there for a while."

Auriol hugged the girl. "You are splendid, Hannah! Thank heavens for the vices of servants. You will be well rewarded for tonight's work, but for now let us waste no more time. Lead the way."

With the master and mistress out and Auriol ostensibly retired for the night there were few servants in evidence and the house was very quiet. When they reached the butler's pantry, Auriol relieved Hannah of her candle, saying, "Remain here and keep watch for me. I will be but a short while."

Crispin Dainton was waiting within. He looked a little uncomfortable at being secreted in so inauspicious a place as the butler's pantry, but his expression of mild irritation gave way to one of alarm when he saw Auriol.

At the sight of Crispin's blond and fresh good looks Auriol knew without any doubt that she could not marry the Duke whatever the cost to her reputation. In an instant she had compared this man's romantic appearance to the dark, satanical looks of Hampden. She compared his smile to the cynical sneer of the

Duke, and giving a cry of anguish, she threw herself into her young suitor's arms.

"What is it, my love? What has alarmed you so thoroughly? I was full of anguish to receive your note and yet I was bewildered by it too. You should have been at Lady Hartington's tonight; I was on my way there myself when your note arrived.

"What is it that threatens your very life, my love? Only tell me."

Auriol extricated herself from his welcome embrace and made an effort to be rational. "My step-father received an offer for me today," she told him breathlessly, "and he accepted on my behalf."

The colour drained from his already pale cheeks. "Who?" he asked in a whisper. "Perivale? Compton? Not Lloyd, surely?" She shook her head.

"None of those paying court to me."

"Then who?"

"The Duke of Hampden."

Crispin Dainton turned away from her. "My God," he whispered. "How can this be? To my knowledge he has never so much as glanced at you."

"Not even a call," she added mournfully.

The colour was fast returning to his cheeks. "How dare Mr Ardmore accept him without consulting your wishes!"

"Who would not accept a duke?"

"He is penniless ... dissipated. Oh, I can scarce bear to think of it without shuddering. The very thought of it ... him ... reviles my sensibilities. What can Ardmore be thinking of?"

"As my mother pointed out, Crispin," she said in a

voice shaking with emotion, "he is a duke for all that."

Mr Dainton put one hand to his head as if it ached abominably. "Oh, Fate, why are you so unkind to me?"

"Crispin, if only you had offered for me first!"

"It would have made no difference. Your step-father would have had me thrown out of his house for my impudence if I had broached the subject. I'm a third son of a country parson who is no fitting husband for such as you. No, you are worthy of far better."

She put one hand on his arm. "I would willingly be your wife."

"Do not torture me further," he moaned.

"I want to marry a man who loves me not one who loves my fortune."

Crispin Dainton drew himself up straight. "How dare *anyone* disregard your beauty in favour of mere wealth? It is not to be borne."

He caught her hands in his and raised them to his lips. "I always knew I would lose you one day, my love. Yes, I was aware of the impossibility of my hopes from the moment I first saw you, but I could bear it better if you did not love me in return, if I were losing you to a better man who adored you as I do."

Auriol clung on to him. "There is no better man in the whole world than you, Crispin. I cannot marry him. I refuse to marry him. I *will* marry you."

"If only that were possible, but I fear our love must remain a dream, a beautiful unfulfilled dream."

"No, I will not accept that. Can you not do something, Crispin ... challenge him to a duel and kill him?" she suggested, brightening a little.

Mr Dainton drew back from her. "A duel? The Duke of Hampden?" His cheeks paled once again. "He could kill me easily even if he were half asleep or in his cups. He is a far better swordsman than any man I know. Even if that were not so and I did kill him Mr Ardmore would simply choose another husband for you from amongst your most eligible suitors."

"Then there is only one course left to us, Crispin. We must elope."

"Elope?" he echoed.

"Yes, elope," she repeated breathlessly. "Once we are married no one can part us, and if it is done before my betrothal is announced there will be no scandal. The Duke and Mr Ardmore will not speak of their arrangement for fear of ridicule."

The look of horror that had come upon his features began to fade as he considered the possibility with more favour. "What will your step-father do when he finds you are gone?"

"He will not follow us, that is certain. We may have to live in poverty for a short while, but if he does not relent once we are married our living in penury will only bring upon him the most serious censure, for runaway weddings are looked upon romantically, and this he will not tolerate. In any event, once I am of age my money becomes my own, so we need suffer for only a short while."

Crispin Dainton caught her hands again. "I believe we could do it, although it will be fraught with difficulty. We shall not be able to travel in style and you are not used to discomfort."

Auriol laughed scornfully. "What is a little discomfort compared to a lifetime of misery?"

"It will take a deal of organising," he muttered thoughtfully. "It will take a little time."

"We cannot afford time, Crispin. If it is to be done it must be done now, before I am forced to acknowledge Hampden as my future husband. Even that I refuse to do but I cannot prevent a public announcement being made. We must act immediately.

"My step-father will be out for hours yet and no one will know I am gone. I need only a small portmanteau which Hannah can pack within minutes whilst I dress. We can then go to your lodgings to collect your own belongings."

"Tonight?"

"You have a carriage outside, do you not?"

"Yes, indeed. I came as quickly as I could when I received your note."

"Then it must be tonight. I cannot bear to remain here a day longer now, for I have disagreed with Mr Ardmore and I have quarrelled with Mama. I just could not bear to remain, for they will make me relent and receive him tomorrow. It would be unbearable."

She looked at him piteously. "Oh, my love," he cried. "I cannot abandon you to such a cruel fate. We will be well on our way to Scotland before you are even missed."

V

The Duke of Hampden wandered aimlessly between the tables where his acquaintances played faro and hazard. He paused at one table on which lay a diamond necklace. It glittered and winked beneath the great crystal chandeliers; a fortune in gems. At the turn of a card the necklace was lost and the lady who did so showed not the slightest emotion; she merely unclipped her bracelet and set that down too.

The Duke's lips curled into a smile of deprecation. How foolish, he thought, were these people who tried to desperately to recoup their losses. Such tactics could only end in disaster. He, himself, had ample cause to know that.

As a gentleman wearing a high toupee and a purple brocade coat victoriously scooped up the bracelet, the Duke stifled a yawn and he walked on, scanning the powdered heads around him; the women who wore feathers and fruit in their hair and the men in velvet and sequinned brocades who were equally as vain, showing their colourful plumage like peacocks.

As he glanced around he experienced a feeling of disappointment, for the face he wished to see was not present this evening. In his mind's eye he saw her, clear green eyes and dark red hair, and skin that was as white as milk. How men adored her, he thought, all except for one, of course. He smiled again and sighed. Ah well, he would see her tomorrow without fail.

After a while, having had conversation with several people of his acquaintance he decided not to take a seat at one of the gaming tables and began to make his way towards the door. He sought out his hostess in order to make his farewells but instead caught the eye of someone else. A moment later the vision floated towards him. The woman wore a confection of spring vegetables in her powdered and padded hair, her once pretty features were now sadly faded and her cheeks were well-rouged and adorned with various types of patches, none of which became her.

The woman curtseyed low before him. "Your Grace, how delighted I am to see you."

He took her hand and bowed low over it. "Mrs Ardmore, the pleasure is reciprocated most heartily."

At such a warm reception she blushed slightly, for she had had little conversation with this man in the past. "I was sorry to have missed your call today. I was, alas, indisposed, but had I known of your call I would have made an effort to see you."

"Please don't apologise, dear lady. Mr Ardmore and I were in conversation for some considerable time and I certainly did not expect you to receive me after that. However, I do hope to call again on the morrow and see both yourself and Miss Stanford."

Mrs Ardmore fluttered her fan in front of her face in an effort to hide her confusion at the mention of her daughter's name. She almost hated her husband at that moment for forcing her to approach the Duke. In view of Auriol's reaction to the news of her betrothal there was nothing she wanted more than to hide away from him until the matter was resolved, for she could not console herself that Auriol would become reconciled to her step-father's future plans for her.

"We shall look forward to it with pleasure," she answered at last.

"I looked to see her here tonight . . ." he ventured, glancing around him with an air of vague bewilderment.

"Ah," Mrs Ardmore gasped, pausing to seek a plausible excuse for Auriol's absence. Her daughter rarely, if ever, missed a social function and the Duke must be only too aware of this.

"She is indisposed?" the Duke suggested helpfully.

Mrs Ardmore's colour heightened even further and she laughed selfconsciously. "The truth of the matter is, Your Grace, Miss Stanford was quite overcome by the news of her betrothal and the poor child is so beside herself with joy at the prospect of her coming marriage that she was almost in a state of nervous collapse tonight. Even though she so desperately wanted to share her happiness with all her friends and acquaintances here tonight, I could not allow her, in all conscience, to attend the festivities."

The Duke allowed himself a smile. "I quite understand, Mrs Ardmore. You were most wise to dissuade her from attending but I beg you give her my compliments. And now, if you will excuse me . . ."

Isabella Ardmore bobbed a curtsey and with some relief watched him saunter across the room before she returned to her husband's side. She could not help but think, although only fleetingly, that it would have been nice to have a son-in-law with whom she could feel at ease. The Duke, she was persuaded, was a man with whom no woman could feel at ease. He had a way of looking at one that was most disconcerting, as if he knew every thought that went through one's mind, and in these circumstances it was rather more than discomfiting. Suddenly she felt a pang of alarm on her daughter's behalf but it was then that she caught sight of Dorothea Makepiece. All her misgivings faded into nothingness at seeing her friend here tonight, of all nights and, smiling with delight and anticipation, Mrs Ardmore made her way purposefully towards her.

VI

The Duke wandered slowly down the steps and paused to glance at his watch outside Lady Hartington's house. From the place he had just left he heard the sound of merrymaking floating out of every window and open door. He put his watch back into his pocket. It was still early, far earlier than he had intended to leave this particular function, but the evening had not turned out quite as he had wished. He had not seen Auriol Stanford since she had been informed of her coming nuptials, and although he would have given almost anything to have been there when she had been told, he was most anxious to judge her reaction now. Now he had to be resigned to postponing that particular pleasure. He knew a little about his betrothed, and from his conversation with Mrs Ardmore he was certain the truth of the matter was that Auriol Stanford—to be plain—was in one of her miffs.

At the thought of it he smiled to himself and when he raised his hand two chairmen came running towards him accompanied by the link boys. As he settled back into the sedan chair he put all thoughts of his betrothal and coming marriage to the back of his mind, and there, he told himself, they would stay—at least for the next few hours.

VII

"*Mon cher amour.*" Marie Gillray sank back into the silk pillows of her bed and sighed happily. "I thought, oh, so unhappily, that you would not come tonight."

"I did have another appointment this evening but the entertainment was not sufficient to keep me away from you, Marie."

The Duke leaned over and kissed her and then drew away, looking down at her with something like wonder. "You are, Marie, the most womanly woman I have ever known."

"Coming from you, *cheri*, this is indeed a compliment to cherish, for you must have known a great many women in your lifetime."

"You talk as if I were a hundred years old."

She chuckled, "Oh, you do not behave as a hundred years old man, *mon amour.*"

He sank back beside her and stared up at the oyster satin draped over the bed. How many happy hours he had spent beneath that canopy, he mused. It was incredible how no other woman could please him as Marie Gillray had done over the years, although his long residence in France had proved to him that no woman could love like a Frenchwoman.

She turned on her side to look at him and ran her finger provocatively down the side of his face and along his lips. "What is it you are thinking, my love? You look so deep in thought."

"I must talk with you on an important matter," he told her, still staring up at the tester.

"Yes, *cheri,*" she murmured, throwing her arm negligently across him. She was curled against him like a kitten. Her lips were close to his ear and he could feel the warmth of her body so close to his, the smell of her perfume that clung to his body to remind him of her even when they were not together.

After a moment he disengaged her arm and slipped out of bed, drawing on a brocade dressing gown that lay over the back of a chair. He came back then to sit on the edge of the bed as she stared up at him quizzically.

He took her hand in his and gazed at the perfection of her features. The clear blue of her eyes, which reminded him of a summer day, the flawlessness of her skin, and the colour of her hair, like ripening corn.

What amazed him most was her air of youth and innocence which she had somehow managed to retain even though she was, he guessed, older than himself and had lived a life not conducive to retaining either youth or innocence.

"Marie, I have something to tell you . . ."

She sat up in bed, quite unconcerned that the covers remained where they were. "Yes, *cheri*, what is it? Tell me. Don't be afraid. Have you gambled too deep? Are the duns after you?"

He smiled and looked down at the hand he held in his rather than at her. "Its nothing like that. I'm . . . I am to be married very soon."

She drew away from him as if stung. She said nothing. She just stared at him in disbelief, drawing up the covers slowly now.

"I wanted you to learn it from my lips rather than those of gossips who would be only too eager to impart the news to you."

At that her lovely face twisted into a grimace of pain as she realised at last what he was saying to her. "Traitor," she hissed through clenched teeth. *"Mon dieu*, you have betrayed me."

He watched her as she got out of bed and unhurriedly drew a wrapper around the perfect thing that was her body.

"Marie, please understand . . ." he begged.

"You said you would marry no one but me."

"I would if it were at all possible," he told her sadly and truthfully, "but I am penniless and I am sick of living on my wits, my fortune sealed at the turn of a card or a throw of the dice. My father lost almost everything he possessed in that way and I learned my lesson well."

"I hate you!" she cried, shaking her head wildly, and then, picking up a small porcelain ornament she threw it at him. He ducked and it crashed against the far wall, falling to fragments on the carpet below. As he got to his feet another missile came hurtling his way followed by yet another, and each of them were accompanied by a torrent of French oaths which he recognised well. They almost made him blush. He dodged the missiles easily, for Marie's aim was not aided by her temper.

By the time he managed to get close to her there were no more ornaments to hand and so she attempted to claw at his face with her sharpened nails, but he caught her hands in his and threw her down on to the bed, holding her arms over her head so that she could do no more harm.

She struggled like a maddened animal but so slight a creature was no match for his superior strength. She lay there helpless, her eyes flashing murder.

"You must be mad to throw yourself away on some whey-faced heiress who will have the vapours every night!"

"But then I will come to you," he told her logically. "Nothing between us will change, except for my financial circumstances."

Her struggling stopped then and she smiled slowly, her eyes growing soft again. "If you love her I will kill her, Dominic."

"You have no need to commit any crime, Marie."

He let her go and she rubbed her wrists where he had held her. "I cannot bear the idea of you so much as looking at another woman," she said in a piteous voice. "We French women are very jealous. You would do well to remember that for the future."

He took her in his arms once more. "I do not even look at Miss Stanford, Marie."

She laughed delightfully as he kissed her neck. "So

it is Auriol Stanford. I have seen her often in the Park. She rides well and she is always surrounded by a host of adoring *beaux* who vie for her favour. You have done well to win her hand."

"She has a social greaser for a step-father. His interests are his own, not his step-daughter's."

She drew away from him again. "But she is no ill-favoured miss. She is very lovely."

He held her gaze levelly. "Is she?"

Marie Gillray smiled with satisfaction at his answer. "She is very rich also."

"Very." It was his turn to smile with satisfaction.

He made to pull her close to him again but she resisted this time. "When . . . when will it be?"

He let her go abruptly and went round to the other side of the bed. "Within the month I think. I have no wish for delay."

She sighed. "How I hate the thought of it. The marriage may be merely an expedient to you, but I can see her now, waiting for you with open arms, adoring you as only I wish to do."

He was taking off his dressing gown and as she spoke he laughed harshly. "Do not rely upon *that*, Marie. I know more than a little about my bride-to-be and I imagine she is, at this very moment, beating her pillow in fury at unkind Fate who has brought her to my attention."

The Frenchwoman looked at him in amazement. "*Cheri*, I do not understand. You know she will not welcome you as her husband? She has said so?"

"No, we have not discussed the matter."

She shrugged in bewilderment, a wholly Gallic gesture. "Then how do you know . . . ?"

"Don't let it worry that pretty head of yours, my love," he assured her as he pulled on his breeches. "Suffice to say it suits me that she will not relish the thought of marriage to me. In fact I have chosen this moment particularly because she is enamoured by a rather handsome but ineffectual individual by the name of Dainton, a man her step-father would never allow her to marry. Her objection to my suit will be two-fold. She loves him and I am quite convinced she hates me."

He said it with such relish that Madame Gillray shook her head. "Do you not want a wife who adores you? Who will do anything you wish her to do?"

He fastened his shirt carefully, looking into the mirror as he did so. "Not in this instance, Marie. I am told Auriol Stanford has a wild temper and is something of a virago, which will suit me well enough. I should hate Miss Stanford to welcome me as her husband."

He tied his neckcloth and then turned to look at her again. She was still staring at him in astonishment.

"You are taking pleasure in marrying an unwilling wife, Dominic." He made no answer as he reached for his swordbelt and buckled it carefully. "Why? Has she slighted you?"

"Miss Stanford and I have hardly exchanged a half dozen words, which is precisely a half dozen more than I would have wished. You need not trouble yourself as to my reasons, Marie. Our relationship can only be improved by a lack of financial restraint although there will be a short period following the marriage when I may not be able to see you as often as usual, but that will be a merely temporary matter." He reached for his coat and put it on. "That is all which needs concern you, my dear."

"You concern me, Dominic. You are taking delight in the very thought that she will be marrying you against her wishes."

" 'Tis a commonplace enough occurrence."

"But to glory in it is not commonplace." Her eyes narrowed shrewdly. "There is something more to this matter than you wish to tell me."

He drew a sigh, took a pinch of snuff and looked at her across the room. "Yes, there is more, Marie, and I have no intention of telling you about it, but do you recall the time I bought Cassandra?"

Her eyes opened a little wider. "The filly you gave to me?"

He nodded, straightening the lace at his cuffs. "Cassandra, you will recall was the wildest of the bunch."

"She kicked you which decided you on her finally. You said you liked a filly with some spirit because it was more fun to tame her." He met her eyes levelly and she gasped. "Oh, you are a devil. A devil."

He smiled as if she had flattered him. "It is not the first time I have been called that, nor, I fancy, the last."

She slid off the bed again. "Why are you going so early, Dominic?"

"I must—tonight." He smiled ironically. "I am to make a morning call on my future bride and her mama, and it would not do to be late."

As he took her in his arms again she murmured, "She has a look of a hauteur, but she is still a child for all that. Whatever your reasons for marrying her, Dominic—and I know that there is one apart from her fortune—I pity her. I pity her from the bottom of my heart."

He drew her head back so he could look into her eyes. "You have no heart, Marie. None at all, but she will need your pity. Yes, indeed she will."

VIII

Isabella Ardmore arrived back at her home in high spirits. Septimus had won several hundreds of pounds at the gaming tables and therefore was in high spirits himself, and Isabella had enjoyed a rare occasion of being the centre of attention whilst boasting of her daughter's advantageous betrothal.

The fact remained that behind her social triumph was a great deal of unease, for Auriol would not, her mother knew, submit easily to the will of others, especially her step-father, a man for whom she had no love and little respect.

Mrs Ardmore had always grieved at the antipathy between Auriol and her step-father. She supposed it stemmed from the diversity of their respective natures. No two people could be more unalike.

Isabella Ardmore had entered into two not entirely successful marriages to men who were also completely unalike. Richard Stanford had been handsome and dissolute but she had loved him until he died, in a duel fought over some woman. Septimus was quite a different man, she thought, sighing slightly. He was far from handsome and in no way dissolute; he was pompous, she supposed, and had a great regard for his social standing, but he took his responsibilities as a father and a husband very seriously. Richard had cared too little for convention and Septimus too much.

Auriol was so much like her red-headed father that Isabella was frightened for her. She loved her pleasures and was headstrong enough to pursue them in spite of convention. In a son it would have been worrying for Mrs Ardmore, but in a daughter, who needs must adhere strictly to a code of conduct, it was very distressing. A girl like Auriol had no need to look for trouble; trouble would undoubtedly seek her out and she would meet it head on.

Perhaps, Mrs Ardmore comforted herself, Septimus was correct in assuming the Duke would deal properly with her. Isabella hoped so, for Auriol needed someone to discipline her. Crispin Dainton, even if he were eligible, would never be able to do that. But the Duke, she pondered uneasily . . .

"You will have to inform Auriol to be on her best behaviour when the Duke calls," Septimus informed his wife as they entered their house on their return from Lady Hartington's rout.

"Oh dear, I do hope she will receive him civilly."

"You must endeavour to see that she does," her husband told her in severe tones. "She has never yet done my bidding but I am determined on this score. She must obey me on this matter and even your daughter, Madam, cannot refuse. A husband is what she needs and the Duke is the right man for her, there is no doubt about that."

"Yes dear, I am sure you are right." She hurried towards the stairs. "I think I shall look in on her before I retire. She was so very distressed this afternoon."

"As you wish," he answered as he went towards the library. "Personally, 'twould be best to leave her until the morrow. By then she'll have had time to reflect upon her good fortune and be ready to apologise to me."

Isabella Ardmore ignored for once her husband's observations and advice. She had no intention of leaving her daughter until the next day; by then Auriol would have worked herself into such a lather of indignation there would be no reasoning with her at all.

It was only a few moments later that Septimus Ardmore, about to pour himself one last drink before retiring, heard the evening quiet rent by a shrill scream. He hurried out of the library to investigate the disturbance, only to be met by the sight of his wife who was stumbling down the stairs, forgetting elegance and poise. The leaves of her headdress waved dangerously and some fell to the floor leaving a trail behind her. In her haste Mrs Ardmore held up the skirts of her gown to reveal a pair of thick ankles clad in white silk stockings.

"Isabella!" her husband cried, "Control yourself. What is the meaning of this outburst?"

As an answer she waved in her hand a piece of paper and when she reached the bottom of the stairs she tottered towards him unsteadily.

Mr Ardmore was no longer indignant; he was now alarmed. "My dear, what is wrong?" he asked, realising at last that his wife was not merely having the vapours for no good reason.

By way of an answer to his question he received only a half hysterical garble of which he could make no sense, only recognising his step-daughter's name being mentioned several times. He hurried forward to meet her and automatically held out his arms as she began to sway, and when she reached him at last she could only say "Auriol" and then fainted into his waiting arms.

Not knowing what to do Mr Ardmore called for the footman to aid him. Together they carried the swooning woman into the drawing room and laid her on a couch. Mr Ardmore fanned his wife whilst the footman put taper to candle and lightened the room. It was somewhat to his relief that his wife's maid arrived at that moment with her mistress's vinaigrette.

A grateful and bewildered Mr Ardmore left his wife in the experienced hands of her ladies' maid and went to retrieve the piece of paper which remained in the hall where it had been dropped. He snatched it up and in a few seconds it took him to scan the contents his colour rose considerably in his cheeks.

His wife, recovering from her swoon, heard his bellow of rage and groaned loudly. She pushed away the vinaigrette as he came storming into the room, waving the letter before him.

"Oh Septimus," she cried, "the wretch. The ungrateful girl. She has even taken Suki with her. What are we to do?"

She sank back into the cushions. Her husband was

too angry even to speak at that moment. Both of them could readily picture the ridicule they would now suffer when the news became public. There were few people at Lady Hartington's rout who were not informed of Auriol Stanford's betrothal to the Duke of Hampden, and by tomorrow the news would be all over Town.

Mrs Ardmore would not be able to face her friends or attend any assemblies, and her husband could readily see himself staying away from his clubs for an indefinite period.

"Ran away," said Mr Ardmore in a strangled voice at last, with these ghastly visions in mind. "Ran away with that insolent puppy, Dainton. After all I have done for her and she not even my own child."

"I am so sorry, Septimus. So sorry," moaned his wife.

" 'Tis all my fault. I have always been too lenient with her; I see it clearly now."

Her husband stared down at her. "I wish to heaven I had never set eyes on either of you, Isabella. She has always been the sorest trial to me. My only consolation is that Dainton will find this true also."

Isabella Ardmore cried out in anguish as he stormed from the room. "Septimus, how will we face the Duke when he calls upon us tomorrow?"

He paused in the doorway, she had never seen him so angry. "I for one do not fancy the task of telling him. I shall take a coward's course and write to him immediately and hope that he will be too disgusted to come and see us."

"Need we tell him so soon?" she murmured. "Can we not wait a while?"

"There can be no advantage in delaying. The humiliation is bad enough but must be worse if the Duke discovers your daughter's treachery if he is told of it by someone else."

She struggled to sit up whilst her maid watched her worriedly. "Can you not go after her and bring her back, Septimus, before anyone learns of it?"

Septimus Ardmore drew himself up indignantly. "I would not stoop to such folly, Madam. Your daughter has made her choice; I have washed my hands of her for good. That puppy has no sense at all. He will squander her fortune within a year, but she need not come back here for help, for she will not receive it."

"Oh, Septimus," wailed his wife. Plump tears began to roll down her face, cleaving a pale course down her rouged cheeks, and as he walked from the room she collapsed into the cushions, sobbing heartbrokenly.

IX

When the Duke arrived back at his house in Park Street one sleepy footman struggled to his feet and stifled a yawn. When he had received his master's hat, cane and gloves he then held out a silver salver on which rested a letter. "This arrived but a few minutes ago, Your Grace. The messenger said it was most urgent and was to be presented to you on your return however late the hour."

The Duke looked at it suspiciously and then frowned as he tore it open. The footman did not flinch at the oath uttered by his master; he was fully accustomed to His Grace's language when displeased or in his cups.

He read the letter through and then threw it down in disgust. In his wildest fancies he had not imagined this twist of Fate.

He paced the floor of the hall for some few minutes,

his brow creased into a frown of deep concentration. Then he stopped, looked at the footman and said, "Fetch Bennet to me, and then Harding. Send them to the library as soon as you can."

The footman hastened to obey and the Duke strode impatiently into the library to wait the arrival of his valet and his coachdriver. As he waited he examined closely a map of England which hung on the wall. He traced a line with his finger and then grunted with satisfaction.

Bennet, his valet, arrived first. "Bennet, pack a portmanteau for me," he said without preamble, "with just the bare essentials. And then prepare yourself for a journey."

Bennet had been in the service of the Duke for many years and was used to the vagaries of his master's nature, but tonight he was visibly taken aback.

"Tonight, Your Grace?"

"Now," snapped the Duke.

"Do you wish to change into travelling clothes, Your Grace?"

"There is not enough time."

The coachdriver entered the library at that moment and the valet hurried to obey his master's orders.

"Prepare my curricle, Harding, and two of the fastest horses in the stables—the chestnuts, I think."

Impassively the man said, "Yes, Your Grace. Shall we be travelling far tonight?"

The Duke drew in a sharp breath. "Not far tonight, I fancy.

"I shall drive and you will accompany me, not Stephens. I shall need the services of a driver if everything goes according to plan."

The driver bowed his assent and was gone only a moment when Bennet reappeared dressed for travelling and carrying a portmanteau together with his master's caped driving coat.

As he helped the Duke into it he was told, "What happens tonight, Bennet, must remain a secret known only to those of us involved."

"Naturally, Your Grace."

The Duke allowed himself a smile and then slapped the man on the back. "I shall entrust you with some instructions and a letter, Bennet. When I reach my destination it will be for you to deliver it and see that my instructions are carried out to the letter. Is that understood?"

The man's expression remained immobile. "Perfectly, Your Grace. Everything shall be as you wish it."

There came the sound of hoofbeats on the driveway outside. "Good man. I shall write the note now and then we shall be gone with no more delay."

X

Auriol felt cold. She had undressed but still wore a wrapper over her bedgown. She glanced around at the low ceiling and the cobwebs she espied attached to the beams. The whitewash on the walls was years old and was now yellow and peeling, the curtains showed signs of tatters and Auriol shuddered with distaste. She'd had no idea they would come to such a place.

Her bones ached with fatigue and yet she delayed climbing into bed, for she was certain the sheets would be damp and none too clean.

It seemed a long way now from Mount Street, from a house that in retrospect seem palatial. Auriol shuddered and huddled closer to the fire. Mama would have read the letter by now, or perhaps not until morning. By now she would know everything unless she slept blissfully unaware of her daughter's elopement. The thought of that depressed her even more.

But, she told herself firmly, she must not be faint-hearted. This temporary discomfort was worth a lifetime with Crispin; a lifetime with a man who loved her as deeply as she loved him.

Hannah was busily folding away Auriol's clothes and when she had finished she came across to her mistress. "Is there anything I can do for you, ma'am, before you retire?"

Auriol sadly shook her head. "You may retire to your own room now, Hannah. You have had a long day." She raised her eyes to the girl's. "You have done very well."

Hannah's plump face dimpled. "I just want to see you happy, ma'am."

"And so you shall."

"Will you get into bed now? You look chilled and very tired. There's a brick warming it."

"Soon, Hannah. I'll sit up a while yet."

The girl went towards the door and then hesitated, looking troubled again as she had from time to time since leaving London in that furtive way. "I'll stay with you if you wish, ma'am. If you'd like me to be near at hand."

Auriol smiled at such devotion. She wondered then what she had done to deserve it, for she had not always been the most patient of mistresses. She picked up the spaniel and cradled her in her arms. "Suki will protect me, if it's protection I need, Hannah." She frowned suddenly. "I did do the right thing in running away, didn't I?"

The girl shook her head. "That's something only you can know, ma'am."

Auriol sighed. "You're right, I suppose. Only I

keep thinking of Mama. Mr Ardmore will make her life even more miserable now; I hadn't thought of that before. If I'd married the Duke he would have been kinder to her," she added wistfully.

"Beggin' your pardon, ma'am, it's your life you're leading."

"Of course," Auriol said briskly. "Mama would not really like to see me married to such a brute of a man." And then she asked hesitantly. "Have you ever been in love, Hannah?"

The girl blushed. "Lor', no, ma'am, nor should I want to be if this be the result."

Auriol laughed. "How wise you are, Hannah! Goodnight. Sleep well. I know your quarters are not very salubrious but we shall try for better tomorrow night."

The girl picked up her candlestick. "Goodnight, ma'am."

When she had gone Auriol was sorry she had sent her away. Suki squirmed out of her arms and went to curl up in front of the dying fire once more.

It was not really cold; Auriol just felt chilled. The night was lonely and more than a little alarming in strange surroundings, and Auriol had never before put herself beyond the pale of accepted behaviour. She thought of Crispin, of his concern and consideration for her and the passion she knew would soon unite them, and that sustained her.

After a while she decided she may as well go to bed. There was to be an early start to the day tomorrow which meant little enough sleep anyway as the hour was already well advanced. She had just taken off her wrapper when there came a knock on the door.

Thinking it to be Hannah she called for her to come in and received a shock to see it was Crispin who had entered.

"I was about to retire," she said a little sharply, taking up her wrapper again in a protective gesture.

He put one finger to his lips and tiptoed in. "The walls are like wafers, Auriol. Keep your voice down."

Embarrassed to be found in her bedgown Auriol clambered into the bed. "Did the landlord find you a room?" she asked in a voice that was a little strained. She wished he would go.

He shook his head. "There are none available tonight. I'll contrive, never fear." He glanced around him and sighed deeply. "I hate to see you in such surroundings, but we must take what we can just now. We must conserve what little money we have between us for the moment and in truth this place is better than a better known inn. There is less chance of being recognised. We must be very careful until we are safely wed."

He frowned at her. "Are you certain Mr Ardmore will not pursue us?"

She sighed. "Quite, quite certain, Crispin. Besides, if he does you are half his age."

The young man blanched. "I wouldn't want to fight him, Auriol."

"You will not have to. He will not pursue us and he is not a fighting man." She yawned. "And now, my love, be so good as to leave me. I am almost asleep already."

"I shall have to sleep in the coffee room which will mean little enough rest for me."

"Take comfort in the knowledge that it will be for tonight only."

He came up to the bed and unbuckled his sword belt. Auriol looked up at him in some alarm, and Suki roused herself and came across to investigate the newcomer, of whom she was not quite sure as yet.

Crispin gazed at her steadily. "Let me stay here with you tonight."

She drew back from him and Suki growled deep in her throat. "I certainly will not. No! It is out of the question. It will be quite improper and you know it!"

He knelt with one knee on the bed and the spaniel began to frisk worriedly about the foot that remained on the floor. "We shall be married 'ere long; what difference do a few days make?" he asked, irritable now.

"A great deal of difference."

"To me too, in these cold and damp inns. It'll be warmer in bed with you." He laughed and she felt uncomfortable. "For heaven's sake call off the dog, Auriol."

"Suki, down, girl."

The spaniel reluctantly obeyed but then jumped on to the bed, sitting as if on guard next to her mistress.

"And just think," he went on eagerly, leaning closer to her, "if your step-father does pursue us and finds us together he will be only too glad to see us wed."

He laughed again and she answered peevishly, "I have already told you, Mr Ardmore will not follow us. He is too fond of his comfort by far, and if you are so concerned about yours not to endure a few uncomfortable nights before a lifetime of bliss, then I shall be sorry I came.

"Now please leave my room."

He still could not take her seriously. Her passion for him had always seemed so great. "Oh, you wouldn't want me to go back down tonight. Not really, Auriol. It's dashed cold down there, and the benches are hard."

Auriol sprang out of bed then, no longer caring about propriety or her state of undress. "Then if you will not leave this room, Crispin, I shall."

He looked at her in surprise. "There is no need; no need." He started towards the door. "If I'd known . . . Auriol. I thought . . ." He looked so crestfallen that she was sorry.

"Crispin, don't be angry," she begged.

"I'm not angry. You trusted me enough to accompany you. We are to be married."

"Yes," she sighed.

"Oh, darling," he said, coming towards her again, " 'tis my love for you that makes me impatient. I have waited so long for you and nearly lost you. Do you not feel that impatience too?"

All Auriol's indignation melted. "Oh, yes, Crispin, of course I do. You know I do, only . . ."

She had no chance to finish what she was about to say, for there came a knock on the door which made her freeze. Crispin swore roundly and strode over to the door.

He looked at her and smiled reassuringly. "I asked the landlord to send up some supper."

She stiffened again. "Crispin, you had no right to." She shrank further back into the room. "Send him away."

The young man laughed. "Don't be bashful, my

love. No one knows us here. You are Miss Smith and I am your brother."

Nevertheless Auriol moved to where she could not be seen from the doorway. She heard Crispin make some exclamation and then there was an odd sound rather like a dull thud. After a moment or two of silence she went hesitantly forward and cried out in alarm then at the sight of her beloved unconscious and stretched out across the doorway. She ran to him calling his name frantically over and over again.

"He will not answer."

She looked up to see the unmistakable figure of the man she was so desperate to escape.

"Hampden." Her voice was so low it could hardly be heard. She blinked her eyes quickly but when she opened them he was still there.

She stumbled back into the room as he stepped unconcernedly over Crispin Dainton's inert form. Auriol continued to back away from him, wondering if she were in the grip of a fantastic nightmare. How had he come to be there? It just didn't seem possible.

"What have you done to him?" she asked fearfully.

"Not very much," he answered, looking around him in distaste. "I didn't even have to unsheath my sword."

Auriol had gone as far as she might and now stood with her back to the wall watching him fearfully.

"What are you going to do?"

His eyes came to rest on her and, aware at last of her state of undress and the compromising circumstances in which he had found her, she blushed to the roots of her hair.

"I am going to take you out of here, of course. I can think of no other reason why I should suffer the discomfort of a night journey." He walked over to the bed and pulled back the covers. "Ye Gods, what a place! Could he not find somewhere more fitting for the woman I assume he hoped to make his bride?"

By way of an answer Crispin Dainton groaned. Automatically Auriol went to him but the Duke put his hand out to bar her way.

"We cannot leave him there," she protested.

"You are right," he conceded, "although I am sorely tempted to."

He went across to the semi-conscious fellow and as easily as if he were a baby he heaved him on his shoulder and carried him to the bed, laying him, none too gently upon it.

"I fancy he is where he wanted to be, although, I'll wager, not quite in this way."

He looked up at her and she blushed again. Crispin groaned and began to move and this time Auriol did run to him, and the Duke made no attempt to stop her.

"You have injured him sorely," she accused, smoothing his brow lovingly, pushing back a lock of golden curls from the bruise now becoming apparent.

"Not as much as I was tempted, Miss Stanford. Now, be pleased to get dressed."

She looked up at him sharply. "Why?"

"We are leaving."

His tone denoted an endless patience that was deceiving, and Auriol, at such a peremptory order, stiffened.

"I have no intention of leaving here tonight, and certainly not with you."

His eyes burned into her. "You will, Miss Stanford,

you most certainly will even if I have to carry you out on my back dressed just as you are now, which will give the landlord and his lackeys some amusement."

Auriol knew it was no idle threat. Moreover he would enjoy doing so and her eyes swam with the tears she was determined not to shed in his presence.

"I cannot leave Mr Dainton as he is. He needs nursing."

"He will soon recover," he answered smoothly. "I assure you I hit him very gently, but I can, if you demur further, hit him with more force."

"You would not!"

"I assure you I would."

She had already realised he was not a man to issue idle threats. She swallowed a cry of anguish. "Where are we to go at this time of night?"

"That you will discover when we arrive."

"I am too tired to travel further."

"You will not rest easy here."

He picked up her gown and held it out to her. Slowly and unwillingly she got to her feet and as she took the gown from him she met his eyes. They mocked her and she knew he was enjoying himself hugely at her expense, and not for the first time did she ask herself why it was she out of all the women he might have chosen for whom he had offered.

"My maid . . ." she began.

"Already on her way in my curricle," he answered and her eyes widened. "She is with my valet. Have no fear for her; she will come to no harm unless she proves to be as stubborn as her mistress."

Auriol's eyes opened wide with the horror of a new realisation. "But I cannot travel alone with you."

He threw back his head and laughed, which caused her fear abate and her anger to kindle once more.

"You are late in becoming conscious of propriety," he said at last. "However, I admire it in you, even if it is of no account after what I found here tonight. Do not delay further; I am already impatient to be gone, and when I grow impatient I am not a pleasant fellow."

Auriol drew herself up to full height, which meant that she almost reached his shoulder. She knew, at the same time, that it was difficult to appear dignified in one's nightclothes and frustration almost choked her.

However, she said with some vestige of dignity remaining, "Be pleased to leave the room, Your Grace, whilst I dress."

At this he began to laugh again. "Oh no, Miss Stanford. I have no intention of allowing you a chance to escape me again, or to barricade the door when I go out. You will remain within my sight until we are in the chaise, which I am happy to say your . . . lover was kind enough to hire. He will, I fear, find it a far walk to London on the morrow."

Auriol's face contorted with fury at his impudence and far more at his amusement. She could bear most things with good grace, but not being laughed at by a man she detested, a man who was undoubtedly the victor of this particular imbroglio.

Without thinking she tried to slap him for his impudence but her intention was so clearly marked upon her face that he managed to smile as he caught her hand. He held her wrist in a grip like a vice and they stared at each other for a few moments before Auriol attempted to extricate herself. But still he held her, drawing her towards him with deliberation and kissing her fully on the lips. After a moment or two he drew back, smiling at her triumphantly, and Auriol, so angry as to be beside herself, spat full in his face. The smile disappeared and his face twisted with fury, and then he pushed her roughly towards a silk screen which stood in the corner of the room.

"If your modesty is so outraged go behind the screen, but if you are a second longer than I deem necessary I shall come in and fetch you out whatever your state of undress."

Auriol stumbled towards the screen with the force with which he had propelled her and she cried out in vexation. The rough feel of his lips were still on hers and in a useless effort to erase it she scrubbed at them with her fingers.

Behind the screen she began to dress hastily, for she did not doubt he would welcome an opportunity to humiliate her further on only the smallest of pretexts. He was far more wicked and depraved than she had previously thought.

Her fingers were trembling and the hooks seemed to elude her time and time again.

"How did you find us?" she asked breathlessly, hoping he would not notice the time it was taking her to dress.

" 'Twas easy," he boasted. "There was only the one road you could have taken and I was aware that a lady of your kind, Miss Stanford, could not endure the rigours of an all night journey. Besides, hired horses are not of the best. This was only the third hostelry I enquired at. I must own, Miss Stanford, your lover could have chosen better."

"He thought if it were not such a fashionable place there was less chance of being recognised."

"Ah, now I understand. It would not have occurred to him that by the time any report on you was made in London you would have long been gone.

"Are you ready yet, Miss Stanford. I am growing impatient."

She was pulling on her stockings. "Not yet," she answered hastily. "You should not have sent my maid away. I am unused to dressing myself."

"I would be pleased to assist you if you need it."

Auriol cried out in alarm and to her further chagrin he laughed again.

"You are a fiend," she cried. "My step-father must have been mad to accept you."

"Not mad, Miss Stanford," he answered mildly, "simply anxious for a step up the social ladder. 'Tis a natural aspiration."

"Did he send you after me?"

"No, it was my own idea entirely. I had no fancy to have it known my betrothed had eloped with another man."

"Your pride is excessive."

"The Seymour pride is known to be so."

"Even so, I wonder that you condescended to trouble yourself over me. After all you would have soon found another Papa only too anxious to make his daughter a duchess."

"No doubt, but it was you whom I wanted, Miss Stanford." She glanced over the top of the screen and saw that he was sitting on the end of the bed with his back towards her. He was still wearing his evening clothes but he had discarded his wig and wore his hair tied back with a ribbon, which indicated that he had left his home with the utmost haste.

"Shall we be going back to my step-father's house?" she asked.

"He would not have you. It need not concern you where you are bound, Miss Stanford. You are so thoroughly compromised for it to be of no matter at all. You are an unfit wife for any gentleman. No doubt Mr Dainton would still have you, for it was he who compromised you and you are still an heiress, but I am afraid he will not be allowed to do that."

Auriol gave a little cry of alarm. She had not thought of her reputation, for it was to be only a matter of time before she would be wed to Crispin. Now that was impossible. What was to become of her? The Duke of Hampden would have no pity on her now.

She peered over the top of the screen again. Crispin was still insensible on the bed. The Duke glanced at his watch and as he put it away he said, "You have one more minute, Miss Stanford. Then I come in to get you."

She came out slowly and as quietly as she could. Her eyes sought and found an empty wine bottle which stood on a table by the bed. Her hand fastened around it and she tiptoed towards the Duke. She had to clutch it in both her hands to stop the thing shaking about, but still when she raised it she was unsteady in her action. Just as she was about to bring it down on his head with all her might he turned and saw what she meant to do. The look of surprise on his face stopped her and before he could spring to his feet and dash it from her hand the bottle had slipped from her fingers to shatter on the floor at her feet.

She turned away from him and buried her face in her hands. "I hate you," she sobbed.

"You have already made that abundantly clear," he answered, "But I warn you not to try such tactics again.

"And now be done with your weeping. I cannot abide wailing females. Your lover could not have considered you so well to incite you to this folly."

"It was my idea. I begged him to rescue me."

He sighed. "I can readily believe it." A moment later she felt her cloak being draped around her shoulders. "Let us not delay further, Miss Stanford, for the horses must grow restless."

She wiped her tears away hastily, hating him to see her weakness. She went across to the bed to look down on the man she loved. He looked just then like a sleeping angel and her heart contracted.

"He is still insensible. There is no sign of life. Are you sure you have not killed him?"

"I did not hit him hard enough to stun a kitten, but I will kill him if you wish it. He deserves to die for the wrong he has done you tonight."

"No!" she cried. "He is no match for you."

He stared across at her. "Nor are you, Miss Stanford, and the sooner you realise it the more easily we shall deal together."

"Never," she vowed fervently.

He held out his hand to her, which she ignored. As she went towards the door he said, "He will have a sore head in the morning." He looked down at Auriol and smiled in a way that made her shiver despite the warmth of the evening. "And that will serve to teach him not to interfere in the affairs of the Duke of Hampden."

Part Two

*If one judges love by
the majority of its effects,
it is more like hatred
than like friendship.*

I

"Wake up, Miss Stanford! Come along now, wake up. We have arrived."

Auriol was jogged out of the comforting sleep of forgetfulness by a rough hand that shook her mercilessly. The hood of her cloak had fallen from her head and her hair was tumbled around her shoulders. She felt as if she had been asleep for hours, and yet she guessed she had slumbered only a short while, for every jerk of the carriage had registered in her slumber.

"Where are we?" she murmured sleepily.

The steps were already let down. When she glanced at the man at her side to her amazement he looked as fresh as if he had just got dressed for the evening, whereas Auriol felt as though she had not slept for days, and she knew that her appearance reflected her feelings only too well. Less than twenty-four hours ago she had cantered in Hyde Park accompanied by her friends, unaware that the beginning of this nightmare was awaiting her return home. How she longed now for that blissful ignorance to be hers once more.

The Duke leaned forward to draw the leather curtains that had assured them of complete privacy. Auriol peered out of the window, unable to hide her curiosity any longer. A moon illuminated the grey castle in front of which the chaise stood. It looked eerie and unwelcoming in the moonlight even though there were lights in many of the windows. Somewhere not too far away an owl hooted.

Auriol felt panic stir inside her. "Where are we?" she asked again in a broken voice. "Where have you brought me?"

"To Hampden Towers," he answered, gazing at her in amusement. "My country estate.

"As luck would have it you were lodging only ten miles away from here. It is almost as if you wished to facilitate me."

She withdrew into the corner once more. "You have no right to bring me here without a chaperon. When my step-father discovers . . ."

"He will say nothing and do nothing, Miss Stanford, for he is a man of great pride and dignity, who, for some reason, fears public ridicule, which will most certainly ensue if it is discovered that you had eloped with Mr Dainton on the day of your betrothal to me. Look for no assistance from him, for it will not be forthcoming.

"Shall we go inside? It is not as comfortable as might be, but better by far than the 'White Goose'."

Auriol know there was no possible escape now. She

had brought this cruel fate upon herself by her rash actions. If only, she told herself, she had paused to think. But then, she reflected sourly, who was to know this fiend, this torturer, would pursue her with such dedication?

She allowed the footman to help her down, refusing the Duke's hand. He followed close on her heels, determined even now that she should not be more than a few inches away from him, but as she paused to survey the medieval facade of Hampden Towers she was unaware that he had come to stand behind her.

Even seeing lights in some of the windows did not diminish her feeling of cold and desolation. It was such a grey building, so large and daunting, and quite unlike the Palladian mansions with their modern conveniences, which belonged to the friends of her step-father. Auriol looked up at the towers which gave their name to the building and imagined them to be ideal prisons for runaway heiresses. He could keep her a prisoner in one of them for an indefinite period; no one would think to seek her there. She had eloped with Crispin so who would possibly imagine her a prisoner of the Duke of Hampden?

"Let us not tarry out here any longer, Miss Stanford," said the Duke, startling her out of her appraisal and her disturbing thoughts. " 'Twill be warmer inside, I fancy, and you are shivering with cold."

In the cavernous hall a fire was lit in the stone fireplace which dominated it. Suits of armour stood in alcoves, silent and sinister watchdogs for generations, and coats of arms and dusty portraits adorned the bare stone walls.

Huddled into a chair near to the fire was a figure

she recognised immediately. As she entered the hall Auriol cried out in delight to see her, and her cry echoed around the hall.

"Hannah! Oh, Hannah, I am so pleased to see you!"

Auriol embraced the girl as she rose to greet her mistress. "Thanks be that you are safe, ma'am. I hardly knew what to think when he," she looked accusingly at the Duke, "ordered me into his carriage. He said it'd go worse for you if I didn't obey him," she added in even more heated tones.

Auriol drew away from her maidservant and sighed. "This is the Duke of Hampden, Hannah."

The girl's countenance fell and she dropped a deep curtsey as he approached them.

"Beggin' your pardon, Your Grace," she murmured, "But I wasn't to know . . ."

"You have aided your mistress in this foolish escapade, girl," he said severely, "and although I am willing to recognise that your reasons were commendable, I must take a very dim view of your behaviour. I trust that you will not encourage her in any folly in the future. If you do I shall be forced to dismiss you and provide an abigail of my own choosing. Is that clear?"

Hannah looked for direction at her mistress, but Auriol simply lowered her eyes and the girl did likewise. "It is understood, Your Grace. I only seek to serve my mistress to the best of my ability."

"Good. You must continue to do so, bearing my warning in mind."

He glanced around him. The hall had filled with servants in the few minutes since Auriol's arrival. The

Duke divested himself of his great coat and when the lackey waited to take hers Auriol drew it closer around her.

"I am still cold."

"As you wish," the Duke said patiently. "Do you require any refreshment?"

"I want only sleep."

He allowed himself a small smile. "Presently, my dear." He glanced around again. "Ah, here is Bennet. Is all in readiness according to my instructions?"

"Yes, Your Grace. The preacher is waiting in the chapel."

Auriol drew back a pace. She had been looking at the valet but now she transferred her horrified gaze to the Duke as he dismissed his servants. Useless to look to them for help anyway. Like every other aristocrat he owned them body and soul, just as he would own her.

Her mouth went dry, her eyes filled with fear. "Preacher," she echoed. "Why did he speak of a preacher?"

The Duke smiled at her again. "Yes, my dear, the preacher is waiting for us. You have caused the poor fellow to be brought from his bed, for our wedding has of necessity been brought forward."

She looked around her in bewilderment and then back to him. "You still wish to marry me?"

"Of course. Did you doubt it?" She blushed and looked away from him. "Did you think I had any other plans for the exalted Auriol Stanford?"

He put one finger beneath her chin and raised it so that she looked into his face. His eyes mocked her again and his lips were curved into a sardonic smile, and she was forced to recall the kiss that had almost burned her lips with its intensity.

"Your charms are manyfold, my dear, as no doubt so many a broken-hearted buck can testify, and in the normal way I should be delighted to enjoy them. But such charms have many women; those who frequent Hyde Park after dusk or the alleyways of Covent Garden. You have an attribute which excites me far more at this moment—a considerable fortune which can only be mine on marriage."

With a cry of agony she drew away from him but she could not escape him so easily. He took her arm in a grip that made her cry out again.

"Be happy, Auriol," he said through clenched teeth, "for after tonight no man would deign to marry you, not even Crispin Dainton if I choose to reveal your stay with him at the 'White Goose'. You would be a social outcast and fortunate to marry an aspiring tradesman, if indeed one such as he would have you. So you may as well consider yourself fortunate in having me as a husband after all."

"I would rather die."

He looked at her in mock surprise. "Not until after the ceremony if you please."

Ignoring her cry of rage implacably he drew her across the hall. "Come along, my dear, let us not keep the preacher waiting any longer."

Auriol began to sob, not in despair, but in frustration and anger. As he pulled her along she buried her teeth into his hand and with an oath he let her go. Without waiting a second she took advantage of his surprise whilst he nursed his injured hand and fled back the way they had come. But Hampden Towers was a maze of stone corridors and in her haste and confusion Auriol took the wrong turning. She knew it almost immediately and in a panic ran back, only to cannon into the man she sought to desperately to escape.

She ran right into his arms and he pinned her against the wall as if she were a helpless butterfly in a fine mesh net. He held her there, both of them breathing heavily and staring at each other in defiance.

"In faith," he said breathlessly after a moment or two, "I had no idea you were such a termagant. It will give me great pleasure to tame you, my girl."

"Never," she gasped.

"We shall see." He gazed at her searchingly as if assessing her anew. "Where, in heaven's name, did you think you could go?"

"Away from you," she said, wearily now. "But I will concede you victory—for now," she added.

He drew away from her and smooothed down the lace on his shirt. Then he offered her his arm. "Let us away to our wedding, Miss Stanford. We have delayed too long already."

Auriol drew herself up straight and tossed her bronze curls away from her face. Stepping past him she ignored his proffered arm and walked, head held high, in front of him.

II

Her eyes were dulled by fatigue and were unseeing as she watched Hannah fold her clothes and put them away carefully. She had eloped in a plain cambric gown which had ironically become her wedding gown. The fine silk one she had intended to be married in remained packed in her portmanteau. Auriol at that moment vowed never to wear it.

" 'Tis a fine house," the girl chattered as she worked. "A very fine house indeed."

Auriol gazed around her. The room she had been given indeed was a fine one with a large anteroom attached. The furniture was shabby and in need of attention but the elegance was not lost; it was merely obscured. Her eyes strayed to the bed which stood on a dias, and then away again. She looked round the walls, the coldness of which was tempered by the tapestries which hung there.

It was difficult to believe that brief cold and emotionless service had made her the wife of the Duke of Hampden. She could not help but think now of all the men she had rejected, men who adored her, who would have worshipped her all her life for herself alone. Each one of them seemed a paragon of virtue in retrospect. She choked back a sob at the memory of the travesty of such a marriage. Loveless marriages were one thing—and commonplace—but hatefilled ones like this quite another.

It was done now and she needs must make the best of it, she acknowledged, although the best could be nothing but misery. She stared at her reflection in the dressing table mirror. Her cheeks were pale already and there were hollows beneath her eyes. How long before her looks began to fade? How long before she became an ill-treated hag? Long before she even came of age, she wagered silently.

She stood up abruptly and pulled the satinet wrapper around her. Even wearing that there was no concealing the shape of her body beneath it. She thought of the Duke's burning eyes looking into her and she shuddered.

"Hannah!" she cried.

The girl turned round. "Yes, ma'am." She dimpled. "Your Grace, I mean."

"Don't call me that!"

"No, ma'am. Not if you don't wish it."

"I don't," Auriol looked at her appealingly. "Did you think to bring some laudanum with you?"

The girl's countenance fell. "Why, no, ma'am. We left so quickly. Are you in pain?"

Auriol twisted her hands together. "Oh yes, Hannah. I am in mortal pain! My heart is breaking into tiny pieces and the pain of it is unbearable."

Hannah came up to her mistress and put an arm around her shoulders. "Oh, ma'am please don't take on so. I don't think the Duke will be unkind to you."

Auriol was trembling violently now. How quickly a happy and fulfilled life could turn into one empty of all but terror.

"He hates me, Hannah. I see it in his eyes whenever he looks at me, only I cannot conceive why it should be so. I knew it was not love that prompted him to offer for me, but this hatred is unreasoning."

Hannah led her mistress unprotesting to the bed. "Now now, ma'am, don't take on so. You will only make yourself ill which will be to no avail. I'll go to the housekeeper and get some laudanum for you, never you fear."

Auriol who had laid down on the bed put one hand out to stay her. "No, no, you must not! You will not be able to get enough for my purpose without arousing suspicion."

Hannah drew away, looking aghast. "Madam, you must not even think of such a thing. 'Tis wickedness even to think of it."

Auriol threw one arm across her eyes. "You are right, Hannah. I will abandon such a plan." Suddenly she swung her legs over the side of the bed and sat up again. "If I were to die now we are wed it would suit him very well. He as much as told me so before the ceremony. Oh, he is so heartless. Well, I shall live on to fight. He may have the right to squander my inheritance on his doxy, but I will live to triumph. You mark my words."

Auriol's eyes flashed with green fire and her maid-servant hardly knew how to answer her. Such disclosures were embarrassing to one in her position, but she was saved the trouble of making any comment, for Auriol waved her hand in the air, saying wearily, "You may retire, Hannah. I am so weary I could sleep standing up."

Hannah looked far from happy at the prospect of leaving her mistress in such a mood of despondency, but after a monent's hesitation did so. Auriol was glad to be alone. Her eyes felt as though they were filled with sand. She felt drained with emotion and doubted if she could ever feel anything again. Even thoughts of Crispin, lost to her for ever, could not rouse her feelings. She was glad of that too.

Hannah had been gone only a few minutes when Auriol was disturbed again. This time she drew back in alarm at the sight of her husband who stood in the doorway.

"What do you want?" she asked harshly, drawing up the covers as far as they could go.

His eyes were very dark in the candlelight. He closed the door and, putting down his own candle, he snuffed it out.

"I am persuaded that no bride could ever have greeted her husband so coldly."

Auriol sank back onto the pillows. Was there no end to his torturing of her?

"Did you expect anything other, Your Grace?"

"Certainly not. You are very predictable in your behaviour, my dear. If you continue in this way there will be few difficulties."

She sighed. "I am so weary I can barely keep my eyes open."

He began snuffing the candles one by one. With each one that was extinguished she sank further away from him. "I shall keep you from your sleep but a short while, Duchess."

He came over to the bed and looked down on her. "I shall hate you until the day I die," she told him.

"I vow you will change your mind."

"Every time I look at you I hate you. Every day that I pass beneath your roof I will detest you even more. I have loved but one man and will love him until the day I die, which I pray will not be long in coming."

He smiled slightly. "But you will live long enough to change your mind, Duchess."

She shook her head and shrank even further away from him. "You can make me do your will, but you can never change my mind."

Suki had taken up her usual place on her mistress's bed but now, sensing that something was amiss, she sat up. Auriol gathered the small animal close to her as if she could protect her in some way.

Without a word he leaned across the bed and took the spaniel from her.

"Where are you taking Suki?" she demanded.

"Into the dressing room. It is quite comfortable and warm in there for her."

Auriol sat straight up. "But Suki has always slept in my bed."

Ignoring her completely the Duke closed the door behind him, leaving Suki to scratch ineffectually at the door. "You are no longer a child," he said severely. "It is time you realised that fact."

He stood there for some moments, looking down on her and as he did so her heart beat unevenly against her ribs. Then with a deliberate action he snuffed out the last candle. Auriol heard the rustle of his dressing gown as he discarded it and then she knew that he was in bed beside her.

She lay there impassively, willing herself not to shrink away from him as his arms drew her close to him. "Do not shrink away from me, Duchess," he said softly. "You are not by nature cold."

"I am as cold as the dead."

"You disappoint me. I had hoped you would not passively accept my advances."

"You are my husband. It is my duty to accept your advances. You may treat me as you will."

"Ah, so you have learned your first lesson well. But even so, you disappoint me, for I had hoped for some resistance from you. You are no milk and water miss to meekly give in to me this way."

Her eyes were becoming accustomed to the dark. She could see him now, the profile of his strong features which were very close to hers on the pillow beside her.

"You really do enjoy pitting your will against mine, don't you?" she said in amazement.

"Yes indeed I do," he told her with a sigh, adding ironically, "It is all a piece of my cruel nature."

She did draw away from him then, to the far side of the four poster. "What kind of a man are you?" she asked in a harsh voice.

He laughed wickedly and Auriol cried out in alarm

as he moved closer to her. His hand caressed her neck gently and she trembled violently beneath his touch.

"I will show you what kind of a man I am, Duchess."

His hand slipped from her neck to the top of her bedgown and before she realised what he was about to do with one jerk of his hand he had ripped it from neck to hem.

She tried to scream out in fear of him but before she could utter a sound his mouth was on hers, forcing open her lips beneath his. She braced herself to receive his assault but it was only moments later that she found she could not withhold herself from him. She felt as though she were drowning, drowning in a warm sea, and as he kissed her in a way she had never imagined it was possible to be kissed, passiveness left her as abruptly as it had come, as unwillingly she allowed his lips to rouse her to a passion she had never yet known. She was sure she would die of it, but death could surely never come so sweet.

III

Auriol woke up slowly. For a moment she could not remember where she was, for the bed felt immediately strange. She turned over sleepily and as she did so her entire body ached as if she had lain on cobbles all night instead of this soft feather bed. She opened her eyes at last and they focused on the damask tester above her bed. She turned again restlessly and caught sight of her ruined bedgown which lay on the floor where it had been discarded the night before.

She gasped in alarm as the memory came to her at last. She sat up, pulling the sheets over her naked body as she did so. The pillow that lay next to hers still bore the imprint of his head, but as her fingers reached out to touch it she realised she was now alone.

Her eyes quickly scanned the room but there was

no sign of him and she gratefully subsided into the pillow again, burying her face in it.

The shame she experienced at that moment was overwhelming; the shame of her own response to his kisses and the gratification she had derived when she had expected nothing but humiliation and pain.

She heard a sound in the adjoining room and froze into immobility. Out of the corner of one eye she saw him standing in the doorway looking at her. He was half dressed, wearing only an unbuttoned shirt and his breeches. As he approached the bed she quickly closed her eyes and feigned sleep.

It was all she could do not to move a muscle as he stood there watching her. She had never been more aware of her own vulnerability. She had always considered herself independent, but now she had to acknowledge that it was all a myth. No woman, however rich or beautiful was ever totally independent. In one way or another they were all a prey to the whims of some man.

"Duchess," he said softly, and his mocking use of her new title roused her to silent anger. "Duchess, I know you are awake."

Auriol turned over and threw a pillow at him which he dodged successfully. Finding the door open at last, Suki came running joyfully to greet her mistress. The Duke laughed and sat down on the bed before her as she hastily pulled up the sheets as far as her chin. Suki jumped on to the bed and he made no attempt to dislodge her.

"Did you sleep well?"

She looked away from him. "Well enough. You are an early riser."

"You seem surprised."

"Nothing about you surprises me."

He laughed again in delight as if she had said something that pleased him. "I always rise early when I am at Hampden Towers. I enjoy a ride before breakfast. Perhaps you would care to join me."

Auriol gave a harsh laugh and sank back into the pillows. "You jest."

"No, I am serious," he answered in mock surprise.

"I never rise before noon."

"You have never before lived for any length of time in the country. In keeping to your bed you will miss many a delight, but it will be as you wish," he added mildly. "It is perhaps as well at this moment. You look a trifle fagged this morning and you must have a care for your looks. I would not wish to have a harridan as my wife."

"You would as lief have a gorgon for a wife if she were richer than I."

He touched her cheek with his finger and she flinched away, recalling unwillingly the embraces she had so eagerly accepted after little resistance such a short time before.

"You are wrong, Duchess. I would have married no one but you.

"But," he went on briskly, "if you do not choose to accompany me you will not see me before dinner."

"That is the first piece of good news I have received in days."

He continued as if she had not spoken. "I am to see my land steward immediately after breakfast and we shall have a lengthy consultation and perhaps a tour of inspection. It is several months since I last visited the country."

"You were never, I recall, one to enjoy the rustic life.

"What are your plans for the future?" she asked bluntly. "For *my* future."

He looked somewhat taken aback. "I have none at the present save for my plans to enjoy the countryside and the company of my charming bride."

"Faddle," she said bluntly. "I must return to Town immediately." He looked at her quizzically, one eyebrow slightly raised. "Indeed? And what business is so urgent that you need to return immediately. Your proposed journey to Scotland would have taken many days, and as many back as Mrs Crispin Dainton."

Auriol gave a sigh of resignation. "I left my ... home precipitously—I hardly need remind you of that—and I brought with me few clothes and other necessary belongings."

He smiled his understanding and got to his feet. "As to that, Duchess, you need not fret your pretty little head. We shall not be entertaining during this sojourn. This is our wedding trip and it is not expected of us."

"I shall still require several changes of clothes."

He smiled wickedly then. "Why, Duchess? I much prefer you as you are."

"Oh, I hate you!" she cried in frustration.

He sat down again and, taking a handful of her tangled curls, he drew her face close to his and with slow deliberation he kissed her, using all the considerable expertise that had so excited her on the previous night. At first she resisted determined not to give in again, but then, unable to help herself, as he persisted, as determined as she, her arms slipped around his neck and she responded to him as ardently as before.

He let her go after a while and as she drew back she was breathing heavily.

"I think, Duchess," he said with satisfaction, "you do not hate me quite as much as you did last night."

Auriol let out a gasp of exasperation which only amused him more. He got up and, reaching for her wrapper, threw it over to her.

"What am I to do with myself all day if I am to be here alone?" she complained.

He was going back towards the dressing room. "Look around your new home," he suggested, pausing in the centre of the room. "It is hardly a showplace but as it will be your money which will restore it to its former magnificence you may as well become familiar with it."

He waved to her insolently and sauntered back into the dressing room where she could hear him laughing with his valet.

At last Auriol was able to give vent to her fury. She jumped out of bed and pulled on her wrapper. She heard him laugh again at something his valet had said and furiously she picked up her powder box and flung it at the closed door. It shattered into a thousand pieces, scattering powder everywhere. Suki jumped from the bed and began to bark with excitement. There was a satisfying silence inside the other room but then a moment later there came the resumed buzz of unconcerned conversation. Beside herself now, Auriol seized upon a brass candlestick and threw that with all her might at the door. She was answered only by the closing of the outer door to the dressing room which indicated that he had gone out and had probably not even heard her attack.

All the anger drained out of her then. She sank down into the chair which stood before her dressing table and, burying her face in her hands, she began to cry.

IV

There was a fine view of the estate from her bedroom window. Beyond Hampden Towers unfolded a vista of open fields where stags and deer wandered unhindered between trees and bushes. Beyond them she had a glimpse of water and guessed there would be an artificial lake. A rotunda too, she guessed, for she could just glimpse the dome of it. Family parties would have gathered there on summer days long gone.

The Duke was riding away from the house accompanied by his land steward and a groom. He looked at ease on his horse and rode well, seeming almost at one with the animal. Auriol realised that she had never noticed his riding skill before on the countless occasions she had encountered him in Hyde Park. She wondered now why he had never caught her attention before, for he was a man who demanded attention, especially from the ladies.

Dominic was his name. She had only learned that too last night. Dominic Farquahar Philip Alexander Seymour; Auriol said his name over beneath her breath. She thought of the way he had kissed her and she shivered slightly at the memory of it.

A stranger. She knew so little of him. He had an infamous reputation with women, although only a certain kind of female, and he was known to be lucky at cards. Rumour had it that it was only such luck which kept the duns from his door.

Much of his life she now recalled was shrouded in mystery, which she conceded might enhance his attraction to some people, but it only served to repel her. Auriol liked what was familiar to her; strangeness frightened her.

He was, undoubtedly, descended from an old and noble lineage but he acted without the manners and modes of most of her acquaintances of a similar rank. He seemed to have a rough disregard for accepted behaviour, preferring to do just as he pleased and be damned to all else, which, if she considered the matter, was a description that could so easily fit Auriol herself.

As she stood at the window she felt anger kindle within her. He treated her too with an easy disregard; in a manner no other man would dare to adopt towards her.

As far as she could recall he had but one living relative and that was his sister, Lady Madelaine D'Ouro, whom she had met on a few occasions in the past. Lady D'Ouro had her brother's dark good looks but on the occasions Auriol had been in her company she had treated her with only the most necessary of civil politeness, giving no more regard to her than had her brother.

Auriol drew a sigh. She was in a pretty mess and no mistake. Moreover, she had no sure way out of it. Last night she had sworn she would hate him for ever; today she was not so sure. She was no longer sure of any of her feelings. Perhaps if he behaved consistently towards her ... but his manner alternated between heartlessness and, at times, the most surprising tenderness.

The Duke, she recalled, would be away until dinner time. Auriol at the thought of it became angry anew at his neglect of her. It was almost as if he was doing it deliberately. But it would give her an opportunity to act; she could order a chaise, she mused, and be in London before she was missed. But then she realised she had nowhere to go. Mr Ardmore would not give her shelter, nor allow her mother to do so, and the Duke would pursue her as he had done yesterday, taking delight in doing so.

"There has to be an answer," she said to Suki. "I cannot live with a man who despises me and abuses my sensibilities constantly."

In reply the spaniel, who was sitting comfortably in her mistress's arms, licked her face. Just then Hannah came into the room and she looked horrified to find Auriol so early abroad.

"I'm sorry, ma'am," she murmured, "truly I am. I did not hear you ring for me."

She looked at her fearfully but the new duchess merely smiled. "Do not apologise, Hannah. You needed your sleep, I don't doubt. I didn't ring for you."

The girl looked relieved. "Now, what will you wear, ma'am. There is little enough to choose from, you know."

Auriol laughed harshly. "It doesn't matter. I shall wear the same gown that I wore yesterday. Perhaps if I wear it constantly the Duke will grow tired of seeing me in it and take me back to London for a new set of clothes." She sighed. "Although I fear the truth is that he will not even notice."

As Hannah began to set out her clothes and toilette Auriol came away from the window, for the Duke was now out of sight.

"Now what am I to do with myself all day, Hannah? I fear I shall be terribly bored. I can only hope that the Duke will soon grow tired of rusticating too. He is, I know, fond of Town entertainments." She thought of Madame Gillray and her lips curved into a scornful smile. The Duke she was sure would not remain long in the country with her when Marie Gillray was still in Town.

She caught sight of her torn bedgown which still remained on the floor and as Hannah began to prepare her mistress's toilette Auriol hurried over to the bed and surreptitiously secreted the gown where it could not be found by the maid.

V

Auriol once again woke up alone the following morning. This time Suki had already presented herself and had fallen asleep on the counterpane. Auriol stroked her gently, fingering the spaniel's silky fur. The little creature had already become accustomed to her new life and surroundings, Auriol realised in awe, recalling how easily the Duke had transported her from the room on the two previous nights. On neither of those occasions had she displayed any of her usual jealousy, for in the past Suki had barked ferociously at anyone who came too close to her mistress and certainly would not suffer passively being forcibly taken from Auriol's side. And yet on these two nights, she had.

Auriol drew a sigh. "It seems he has a way with females, but i' faith I know not what it is."

At that moment a maidservant arrived with her breakfast, followed almost immediately by Hannah who was once again surprised to find her mistress awake.

Auriol ate in a desultory way whilst Hannah went about her duties humming happily to herself as she did so. She too, Auriol observed sourly, was quite resigned to her new situation. But, then, what abigail would baulk at serving a duchess? she realised.

During the whole of her first day at Hampden Towers she had remained in her room, unreasonably smarting at her husband's neglect of her. She knew, in view of the circumstances of her marriage, it was unreasonable to do so, especially as they were residing in the country and the time between breakfast and dinner a short one.

She had toyed with the idea of not attending dinner at all last night, to plead indisposition, but she had an uneasy idea that the Duke would not tolerate her absence and as in every other way since their betrothal would inflict his will on her, and Auriol had no mind for further humiliations at his hand.

She had spent that first afternoon writing letters. One to her mother which she wrote and rewrote several times, and finally completed a long missive which she hoped would breach any rift that still remained. The other letter she steeled herself to write— to Crispin. Auriol found she could barely see the paper for the tears that misted her eyes, but she forced herself to write to him in as an impersonal way as she could contrive, assuring him of her safety and happiness and ending with a fervent prayer for his. She deliberately refrained from mentioning their thwarted plans or the passion she still harboured for him. Sensibly Auriol knew she must no longer encourage his ad-

vances, for instinct told her that the Duke would welcome an opportunity to kill him. She was married to a
man who was, in every way depraved.

"There," she had said to Hannah when she had finished the letters, "I entrust you with these. Please see
that they are dispatched immediately."

"Certainly, ma'am. I shall see to it now, if I may be
excused."

As she hurried to the door Auriol stopped her
again. "Hannah." She hesitated and the girl looked at
her expectantly. "I would be obliged if you could contrive to dispatch them without the Duke knowing of
it."

Hannah's plump face broke into a dimpled grin as
she curtseyed. "You can rely upon it, ma'am."

Auriol turned away as the girl left the room. She
shuddered at the thought of what the Duke's reaction
might be if he discovered that she had written to
Crispin, however innocent her intentions, for in truth
she did not yearn for him. Auriol was sensible enough
to know there was no advantage in doing so; she only
regretted never being able to know the felicity they
might have enjoyed together.

Having decided to go down to dinner, when Hannah returned shortly afterwards, they set about choosing a gown for her to wear from the few they had
brought with them.

"The bronze satin," Hannah suggested, "although it
is not really grand enough for dining."

"The Duke will not notice. I shall also wear my
emeralds, which he will notice," Auriol added dryly,
and then, glancing in the mirror, "As to my hair, Hannah, we shall have to contrive as best we can."

"Never you fear, ma'am," the maidservant assured her, "even without your false hair and your own powder, you will outdazzle any lady who has ever graced this house!"

Auriol gave a shaky little laugh. "I doubt it, Hannah, but I am in dire need of such praise. I fear my husband sees me as only so many sovereigns for his purse, and that is not food for my pride."

Hannah chuckled as she began to brush her mistress's hair. "That may well be so now, ma'am, but I'll wager the time will come when he'll sing quite a different tune!"

VI

"I apologise for the lack of ceremony in my dress," she told him when, surprisingly, he came up to escort her to the dining room, "but I brought with me only the merest essentials."

"You look charming," he answered and it gave Auriol something of a shock to see that in place of the usual mockery in his eyes there was something akin to admiration. "I prefer your hair in that rustic style." Auriol's hand went to the confusion of unpowdered curls. "It is so much more approachable than the style in which it is usually worn."

Although she blushed at such apparent praise (for in truth she could never quite tell his true meaning) she found to her surprise too that the evening passed pleasantly enough. He desisted from derision and spoke constantly of his hopes and plans for his estate now that it was to have an owner who could afford to improve it, pointing out that it was for her to plan the improvements inside Hampden Towers itself.

Auriol forbore to say so, but she found it a daunting task. Never before had she been faced with such a huge commission and so unexpectedly.

After a dinner that was surprisingly well-cooked they retired to the drawing room and the Duke took his port there whilst Auriol was persuaded to play the spinet for him.

"You play well, Duchess," said her husband when she stepped from the dais at last.

Auriol stiffened at his condescension, but did not rise to the bait. She merely inclined her head and said, "I am gratified that you think so, Your Grace. It is generally held that I am musically accomplished."

He smiled, knowing she was irritated and also that she was endeavouring not to show it. He watched her carefully as she crossed the room.

"You do not surprise me by that admission. In every way you make an excellent duchess, as, of course, I knew that you would."

Auriol paused and picked up a pack of cards which stood idle on a drum table. "Will you play bezique with me, Duke?" she asked carefully, swallowing her anger.

He had been provoking her in his subtle way but she had already learned that in quarrels with him she could never be the winner and she had no intention of being the loser.

"I will play but only if you call me Dominic."

She remained with her back towards him. "You do not call me Auriol."

"Only because Duchess suits you so well."

"Then I shall continue to address you as befitting *your* rank."

She turned to face him. He was sitting on one of the brocade couches near to the fire. His head lay on the back of it and one leg swung negligently as it crossed the other as he watched her through half closed eyes. The sensation was rather like that of a mouse who was being watched by a cat who was about to pounce.

She met his eyes levelly and held up the cards. "A game, Your Grace?"

He smiled and sat up straight. "Why not? The evening before us is a long one and we must needs do something to pass the time." As she came towards him he asked, "Are you an inveterate gambler, Duchess?"

She sat down beside him; his eyes lingered on the low corsage of the bronze silk gown she wore, and Auriol felt discomfited by him yet again.

"Within bounds, Your Grace. I am not and never have been an inveterate gambler."

"I am gratified to hear it. Too many fortunes are lost by such folly."

Her eyes met his yet again. "And therefore won."

He smiled grimly and his eyes were suddenly hard. "Oh, indeed, Duchess. Most certainly they are." He held out his hand. "The cards?"

VII

As she dressed the following morning Auriol realised, with a sinking heart, that the past two days might well be the pattern of her future life as the Duchess of Hampden.

Without the constant stream of callers, meeting one's friends and acquaintances in the Park, evening assemblies almost every night, life could be unbearably boring. She was not used to a rustic life and could not bear the thought of spending what might be a very long one at Hampden Towers. After all, she was only just eighteen years old; she could conceivably live for another seventy years or more, and for a great many of those years, so could the Duke.

Auriol sank down into a chair as the enormity of her fate came upon her. The Duke had made no mention of returning to London in the near future and the

Season would be over in a matter of weeks. Then there would be the summer at Hampden Towers too, and from what little she had seen of it, it was totally unfitted, as yet to entertain guests. It might be six months before she returned to London and a social life.

She put her hands to her head. "I shall not be able to bear it!" she cried. But only the four walls of her bedchamber could hear her.

At that moment she knew with certainty she could remain indoors no longer. The Duke had not offered her a horse but in truth she had no fancy for riding alone and because she was still totally unfamiliar with her surroundings therefore she could not possibly know where to ride. So, as soon as Hannah had finished with her Auriol took a shawl and went downstairs.

A footman silently opened the door for her and made to accompany her, only she stopped him. When she went out she stood on the doorstep, enjoying the fresh air for the first time in days.

In front of her, as far as the eye could see, lay the Duke's land, formal gardens enclosed by yew hedges. There were flower beds in abundance, ponds and shady arbours, and considering the state of disrepair of the house itself the gardens were relatively neat.

Although it was only two days since she had first entered Hampden Towers by way of this very door, it seemed so much longer. It was as if she had grown up and old in those two days. The carefree days of youth had gone now and would never be recaptured. She was to all intents and purposes the prisoner of this man to whom she was married, and he was a gaoler she hated, someone who tormented her constantly into uneven combat, a man who could make her melt in his arms and forget the iniquities he had perpetrated against her with only one touch of his lips.

VIII

Auriol knew there was no need for her to return in haste. Again the Duke was out with his land steward. Deciding how best to spend my money, she thought sourly, and then had to remind herself that it was no longer her money. Whatever she had possessed days ago now belonged to him.

She took her time to wander round the gardens. Some early blooms were already flowering, although the blossom, which looked so pretty, was fast falling from the trees. The sight of it caused her to think of Crispin and she wondered fleetingly where he was and what he was doing, before ruthlessly dismissing such thoughts from her mind.

After a while she felt tired, for she had walked some considerable distance from the house, and found a bench to sit upon for a while. She remained there for quite some time, just staring unseeingly into space, until at last she roused herself with the thought that she would have to go back.

She walked back slowly in a desultory fashion, making no haste to return to the place she must call home.

"Is the Duke returned?" she asked the footman when she arrived back at the house.

"Yes, Your Grace. Shall I have you announced?"

Auriol shook her head. "Not just yet." There was a long evening to be endured in his company and this was sufficient for her. "Please direct me to the library; I should like to inspect the stock of books."

The lackey escorted her to the library and left her there. The shelves from floor to ceiling were crammed with tomes. It was a much larger library than any she had yet seen. Apart from the amazing number of books there were several leather chairs, three desks, each with a supply of quills and ink and paper, and a sofa drawn near to the unlighted fire.

Auriol felt at home in this room with its vague odour of musty leather. She realised, for the first time, that perhaps Hampden Towers would not be so large or so daunting if it were filled with people. She wondered too if she and the Duke would ever entertain parties at Hampden Towers, as his parents had once done, as with most couples of her acquaintance, doing their social duty and at other times ignoring each other civilly.

Auriol had grown up knowing her mother's second marriage was not an entirely felicitous one, and unconsciously she had yearned for the love of a man she had sorely missed all her life; the love her step-father had never been able to give to her.

Realising she was beginning to feel sorry for herself again, Auriol thrust aside those thoughts from her mind. She went to inspect the books more closely; not surprisingly there were many volumes in Latin and Greek, and no novels.

As she approached a door which led to another room beyond the library, she paused, for she was certain she heard voices. Suddenly she recognised one as the Duke's and wondered if this was where his study was, and if he were still in consultation with his land steward.

She pressed her ear to the door but could hear nothing clearly, except a raised voice which belonged to a woman. Startled she drew back for a moment or two and then curiosity overcame her scruples. As quietly as she could Auriol eased open the door a fraction. Through the crack she could see the Duke, still in riding clothes, perched at the edge of a desk with one booted leg swinging.

"I assure you, my dear," he was saying, "you are most welcome, only I wish you had warned me of your coming."

Feeling a little bolder Auriol opened the door a fraction more and then drew in her breath sharply when she saw the other person present. The woman who stood before the Duke was clad in travelling clothes, a magnificent plumed hat and fur-trimmed riding coat. Auriol recognised the proud beauty immediately, for she was none other than Lady Madelaine D'Ouro, the Duke's sister.

"You could hardly expect me to ignore your letter and continue about my business, Dominic, as if nothing had happened. I'faith, I was almost too overcome to travel."

"Nonsense, Madelaine. Don't seek to gammon me on that score; you are in no way vapourish. Tell me, has Donald accompanied you? 'Twould be excellent to get in some hunting with him whilst I am here."

"Donald could not come at such short notice," she answered peevishly. "Indeed, I have had to cancel two engagements myself. Now, Dominic, you have put me off long enough; what is all this nonsense you wrote to me about? I refuse to believe that you have married this child."

Auriol stiffened as the Duke laughed. "Do you really think I would indulge in such jest with *you*, Madelaine?"

Lady D'Ouro drew in a sharp breath. "Then 'tis true! I can scarce believe it! Only last week you were on the brink of offering for the chit, but in truth, Dominic, after voicing my disapproval to you, I did not believe you would go ahead and do so."

"Do I not always do as I say? On this occasion, Madelaine, your disapproval was of no interest to me."

Lady D'Ouro twisted her gloved hands together in anguish. "But why the haste?"

He laughed again. " 'Tis a long story, my dear, and perhaps one day I shall tell it to you. For now suffice to say Miss Stanford was so eager to become my wife, there was no waiting."

Auriol gasped in exasperation but fortunately it was covered by Lady D'Ouro's own harsh laughter.

"That is certainly a load of moonshine if ever I

heard it," she said a moment later. "Oh, Dominic, I thought you had long grown out of this obsession."

"You should know me better than that."

"This is such folly!" she cried. "No good can come of it. Can you not see that? You should have left well alone and forgot the follies of the past and look only to the future. You could have married anyone. Dominic, anyone."

"I wished to marry Miss Stanford. Now, be pleased to stop fretting for what is done and cannot be undone."

"How I wish you had realised that before."

"I have achieved what I intended, Madelaine, and I am still here to speak of it. Is that not proof that all is well?"

"No! Today you may smile and feel satisfied with yourself, but there is always tomorrow and the days after that. You have the rest of your life to lead."

"And I shall lead it according to my wishes."

" 'Twill not be so easy, I fear. You just have not looked beyond tomorrow. Auriol Stanford is not a woman to meekly accept her fate. No, indeed she is not. You have taken on far more than even you can cope with."

Auriol pressed her ear closer to the crack after seeing her husband unconcernedly take a pinch of snuff and then brush the specks from his riding breeches with a careless flick of his handkerchief.

"You are quite wrong, Madelaine. The Duchess is already settling down as my wife quite satisfactorily, and may I ask why she should not? It was a fair enough exchange; my title for her fortune; there are many who would make do with less."

Behind the door Auriol was seething with rage at the indifferent way he had spoken of her. It was almost as if he had bestowed upon her a great honour, instead of quite the reverse being the case.

"Many may have done so, Dominic," his sister told him severely, "but not Miss Auriol Stanford as I have seen her. Since you were born I have always thought you the most self-willed person I have ever known, but I'll wager your wife is a contender for such a title, and when two such people marry . . ."

He merely answered with a laugh and said, "Sulphur and tinder create sparks."

"You treat this matter as a jest."

"Yes, exactly as that," he said in a cold voice, "and I am enjoying the joke hugely."

"You may do so now, Dominic," she said and then added, in a tone of such anguish that Auriol felt chilled, "But I fear that it will end in tragedy."

Auriol's heart was beating loudly. She had taken his dislike of her as being as natural as her dislike of him, but somehow she felt now there was more to it than that, and she was puzzled.

She flinched when she heard him stand up and closed the door a little for fear that he would notice it open.

"I trust you will stay long enough to meet the Duchess, Madelaine."

Lady D'Ouro sighed deeply. "Naturally. Where is Her Grace?"

"Wandering in the gardens, I believe. She finds it a trifle dull at Hampden Towers."

"On your wedding trip? That I wager is a poor omen for the future. However, I have brought with me those journals and brochures you asked for. They will give her a wide choice of materials from which to choose the new furnishings."

"That will keep the Duchess occupied and out of mischief a piece," he said with satisfaction. "Now, tell me all the news from London, Madelaine. Has the story of our elopement broken yet?"

"No, but now it will not be long. Perhaps even as we speak here at the moment it is being spoken of."

"I take it that the children are quite well?"

"Young Dominic has a teething cold and Maud has had a sore throat. 'Tis only to be expected after such damp weather as we have had lately . . ."

Auriol closed the door, relieved that they had ceased to discuss her in such vitriolic terms. She waited a few moments to recover herself and then, adjusting her shawl, she went out into the hall again. Only moments later the study door opened and the Duke escorted his sister into the hall.

Auriol stood uncertainly in the centre, feeling self-conscious beneath the cold appraising stare of her sister-in-law, and she was grateful when the Duke came to greet her.

"Ah, Duchess, we have a visitor. My sister, Lady D'Ouro."

The lady was obviously reluctant to drop a curtsey but she did so after hesitating a few moments. The Duke, she was aware, was watching complacently the meeting between the two and Auriol forced a smile to her lips and offered her hand to her sister-in-law.

"This is indeed a pleasant surprise, Lady D'Ouro. Do we dare to hope you will remain with us for some time?"

The woman glanced with uncertainty at her brother who, it was apparent, had no intention of interfering in the meeting between the two.

"A day or two perhaps," she said grudgingly at last.

"Splendid." Auriol did her best to look suitably delighted. In truth she was daunted at the prospect of Lady D'Ouro's company. "You can," she went on in a bright voice, "communicate to me the latest news from Town."

Lady D'Ouro's lips curled into the vestige of a smile. "By now, Duchess, *you* should be the latest news."

The Duke deemed it time to intervene at this point. He came forward to take Auriol's arm. "Is it not time to change for dinner?" he asked. "Madelaine, you must be longing for a rest."

Lady D'Ouro inclined her head. "It was an unexpected journey," she said dryly, "and as such tiring."

The Duke motioned to a lackey to escort his sister to the room allocated to her. Lady D'Ouro curtseyed to them both, deeply, and, Auriol thought, mockingly before following the footman to the stairs.

Auriol followed her with her eyes. She was a handsome woman indeed, black-haired and black eyed like her brother, and a famous beauty before her marriage to the wealthy Sir Donald D'Ouro. Her attitude towards Auriol still puzzled her—it wasn't precisely hate; more like pity—but she found herself liking her new sister-in-law in spite of it. She was very like the Duke in appearance, but she seemed far more level-headed and Auriol hoped the time would come when they could be friends.

She shivered a little as she stood there, dwarfed by

the size of the hall, for she was sure in the time to come she would find herself in need of a friend.

The Duke put his hand on her shoulder, which reminded her of his presence, and she whirled round to face him.

"You are cold, Duchess," he said in a soft voice as he looked down into her face. "You should wear more than a shawl when you go out."

Auriol shivered again. His words were perfunctory, mocking almost, but they created in her a sudden longing for him to be protective of her, to really care if she were cold or not, and her sense of loneliness was heightened to an unbearable pitch, for she knew what she wished was not possible.

IX

Once again dinner was a more comfortable meal than Auriol had anticipated. She wore her only other dinner gown, one of pale green taffeta, and a topaz necklace, not by far the most valuable of her jewels, but her favourite. Instinctively she knew it would be best not to flaunt her wealth before her husband's sister, or remind Lady D'Ouro of the Duke's reason for marrying. It was already abundantly clear that she despised the necessity of such a match.

With the presence of Lady D'Ouro, Auriol was relieved of much of the burden of conversation with her husband, for the Duke and his sister talked of people and places known only to them. Auriol as a result did not feel left out of their conversation. She was grateful that she could concentrate on her meal and therefore she ate far more food than she had done since arriving at Hampden Towers.

After dinner they adjourned to the main drawing room and it was Lady D'Ouro who played the spinet whilst Auriol gladly leafed through the new magazines the Duke had requested for her.

"My sister knows Hampden Towers thoroughly, of course," the Duke told her. "Perhaps you can prevail upon her to show it to you while she is here. You can have no better guide."

He glanced at his sister who stopped playing and came down to join them. Auriol began to murmur her dissent, for she had no real interest in seeing the dusty and unused parts of Hampden Towers, and certainly did not wish Lady D'Ouro to be pressed unwillingly into the task of showing it to her. But Lady D'Ouro did not seem averse to doing so.

"If the Duchess permits me," she murmured.

"Only if you do not mind . . ."

Lady D'Ouro gazed at her disconcertingly for a moment or two, and then said, "It is your home, Your Grace. You certainly need familiarising with it."

"I would appreciate your assistance, Lady D'Ouro. 'Tis a very great task before me."

The Duke laughed. "Do not think you are burdening Madelaine, Duchess. She is very proud of her ancestral home as I am. She will be delighted to show it to you."

"Oh, faddle," was his sister's answer, but she did not deny his words, and Auriol realised that like her brother, she was proud in everything.

X

Auriol rose to take breakfast with her sister-in-law the following morning, after the Duke had departed. Afterwards, armed with the brochures of furnishing materials, they wandered the complete length and breadth and height of Hampden Towers, discovering cobwebby rooms even Lady D'Ouro had forgotten existed.

"Hampden Towers," she explained, "has so often been altered and added to over the centuries that there are corners of it which are easily overlooked."

Auriol exclaimed in delight at the view of almost the whole estate from the windows of the one tower room which was still safe to use.

"Isn't it wonderful?" Auriol exclaimed as she ran across to the window.

The room was devoid of furniture and very tiny, with space perhaps for one table and two chairs.

"I've a mind to make this my sewing room. The light is very good."

"It will certainly be good to have it used again." Lady D'Ouro wandered across to the other window and gazed out. "Dominic and I loved to come here when we were children. We used to act out little dramas of our own making."

Her eyes grew soft and warm at the memory and Auriol attended her with interest, for she had not yet thought of her husband as a human being let alone the child he must have once been.

"We would often hide from our governess up here. Even if she suspected we were here, as she must have done, she would not pursue us, for she was so fat she could not manage to climb the stairs."

Auriol laughed and then her companion sighed. "When we went to live in France I think this was the one place we missed most of all."

Auriol looked at her quizzically. "I had no idea you lived in France."

Lady D'Ouro nodded and sighed again. "It was for some years, and when we returned at last childhood had gone."

She went out of the tower room and down the winding stair, leaving Auriol to stare after her thoughtfully.

Next they came upon the old nursery and Lady D'Ouro was delighted to discover some of her dolls which still lay there forgotten, but just as they had been left all those years ago.

"With fresh clothes," she said delightedly, "they will be as good as new. Maud will love them even though," she added to Auriol, "she has so many toys of her own. The nursery overflows with them, but it would give me great pleasure to see these in use again."

Auriol gazed at her as she gathered the dolls together; she looked so young and happy, so unlike the severe matron who had eyed her with disapproval only yesterday. This transformation made Auriol wonder what the Duke would be like if he allowed his mask of pride and cynicism to slip away. Would he too be young and carefree, and as likeable as his sister?

Whilst Lady D'Ouro selected the dolls to take with her Auriol wandered from the bedroom with its small wardrobe and child-sized beds. She fingered carefully the Duke's hobby horse, its bright paint now sadly faded. Did she want another generation of Seymours to inhabit these rooms? she asked herself. In truth she felt no wish to bring children into this loathsome marriage, but she realised she would have no choice if it was God's will.

"Tell me about the Duke," she said thoughtfully when she returned to her sister-in-law.

Lady D'Ouro looked suddenly embarrassed. "There is little to tell. He is as everyone."

"No, that is not true."

Lady D'Ouro smiled. "Perhaps not. Dominic is an individual. You have already discovered that for yourself. He is my brother and as a brother I know him well, but as a husband, that you must discover for yourself."

"You are obviously fond of him," she said, in a tone which indicated such a sentiment was quite a feat.

"We have always dealt well together. By virtue of our diminished numbers the Seymours are a close clan. I don't always like my brother, I must admit, but I certainly do love him."

She started towards the door, still clutching her dolls and Auriol followed her and said quickly in order to change the subject, "I believe we should renovate the downstairs salons and the main bedrooms first, and leave the lesser used rooms until last."

"That would be the best course," came the answer, and Auriol was not slow to note her relief.

She closed the nursery door carefully. "We shall need to employ experts to renovate the paintings and tapestries, but the nursery can certainly be left as it is for now."

Lady D'Ouro smiled kindly for the first time. "Yes, you may easily do so. You will have sufficient time to renovate that suite when the occasion arises."

Auriol quickly put from her mind the mixture of repulsion and longing she felt at the thought. Children, yes, but not his, she thought in despair. Children were surely meant to be born of love.

"You have a large nursery yourself I believe," she asked politely.

"We have four children." She laughed. "Three girls and one boy. Poor Donald is outnumbered by females, as he so often laments." Auriol could not help but smile. "In fact we are hoping to redress the balance a little, for there will be another child before the year is out."

Auriol was taken aback, for there was no sign of it in her trim figure or any diminishment of her vitality.

"You are," Lady D'Ouro, told her, "one of the first

persons to know. Even Dominic has not been told as yet."

Auriol was moved at her confidence. "You honour me, Lady D'Ouro."

"Well, we are related, are we not?"

Auriol put one hand on her sister-in-law's sleeve as she made to move away. "We are related but can we not be friends also, Lady D'Ouro?"

Madelaine D'Ouro gazed at her intently for a moment or two and it was not lost on Auriol that she was now asking quite humbly for that which she had always considered her right.

Suddenly the older woman's face broke into a guileless smile which illuminated her face. "I think that we shall be great friends, Auriol."

Quite spontaneously they hugged each other and then together they went arm in arm to complete their inspection of Hampden Towers.

XI

With the help of Lady D'Ouro Auriol decided upon new schemes for some of the shabbier public rooms and it was decided between them—for the Duke had said, "Do not involve me in women's work"—for several pieces of furniture to be brought down from the attic to be repaired and recovered. Amongst them was a writing desk which Auriol coveted for her own and several handsome chairs which would do well in some of the rooms she considered under-furnished.

It was arranged that extra help was to be engaged to set about the cleaning of the house from attics to cellars, and experts were engaged from London to restore those remaining treasures to their former glory. Within three days the orders for new materials had been dispatched and the work was well in hand. When the ordering was completed both Auriol and her sister-in-law felt that Hampden Towers would soon be fit to receive the King himself. After the orders were given and the work set in motion there was little for either woman to do except inspect the progress from time to time, which was not really sufficient for Auriol, for she had discovered that she was beginning to enjoy being the mistress of her own establishment, especially such a grand one as this, and she actually wished for more to do.

The feckless pleasures of the Social Round had once been sufficient to employ her fully, but now she had found a deeper satisfaction.

"It seems I can hardly venture a pace or two without tripping over some creature who is scrubbing, brushing or polishing something," the Duke complained one evening.

Lady D'Ouro smiled conspiratorially at Auriol who was busily embroidering handkerchiefs. "It is what you wanted, Dominic. Just think how handsome it will all look when the Duchess is finished."

"I could not have done it without your assistance," Auriol said quickly, eager now not to take all the credit.

"I'm sure you could."

"Shall we say you deal well together," the Duke suggested, and they all laughed merrily.

"Neither of you have seen the light of day since your arrival, Madelaine," he went on a few moments later, looking at them both gravely.

"We have been too busy, dear."

"Well, now it seems that you are not and I insist that you both leave the work to those employed to do it and come out with me tomorrow."

"What a splendid idea!" his sister agreed. "A good

canter is what I should really enjoy just now. I shall ride Domino, as always, and Auriol will enjoy riding September."

Auriol put down her sewing and looked in horror, first at Madelaine and then at the Duke. "But, Madelaine," she said in a shocked whisper. "You cannot."

Suki who had been playing with one of the Duke's old shoes in front of the firescreen, sensing something in the air, stopped and sat up in anticipation.

The Duke looked up from his newspaper too. "Why ever not? Madelaine is as fine a horsewoman as I've ever met. Better even than you, Duchess, and you have a good seat."

His sister looked sheepish. "Your wife, I think, is concerned for my health."

He looked at her blankly. "Your health, Madelaine? Are you not well?"

"I am very well, Dominic, but there is to be another happy event in the D'Ouro household." Then she looked at Auriol. "Never you fear, my dear; I always ride when I'm in this condition. I did it before the other four were born with no mishap whatsoever."

She smiled happily at them both but to her surprise her brother merely frowned and buried his head in his newspaper again.

XII

The following day was one of glorious spring weather when the three of them set out for a ride over the Duke of Hampden's estate. Auriol had noticed that Lady D'Ouro often contrived to make her brother laugh and it was not the harsh laughter which he always directed towards her, but it was natural, carefree laughter and when he laughed thus Auriol wondered at the change in his manner. He seemed so very far removed from the man she had married, quick to anger, sarcasm being his only mode of speaking, and she realised he was only the dark, angry young man towards her, and not for the first time did she wonder what she had done to earn his hatred.

During their ride Auriol found she was enjoying life far more than she had for a long time. There was a simplicity about life in the country that was beginning to appeal. There was no need to be constantly on show during the unrelenting round of the Season, and she found this informality relaxing to say the least, and now that she could actually see her planned improvements to the house taking shape, it was particularly satisfying to be at Hampden Towers.

She was shown the remarkable extent of her husband's lands and enjoyed the deference shown to her by those incumbent upon the Duke.

It had been an enjoyable afternoon but as they made their way back for dinner Lady D'Ouro announced suddenly, "I shall go home tomorrow. I have stayed far longer than I had intended."

Auriol was immediately woebegone. Her horse trotted between Domino and the Duke's stallion, Emperor. "You cannot go so soon, Madelaine."

"I have been here almost a week!" Lady D'Ouro answered with a laugh. "I do have my family to attend to, my dear, and, in truth, I miss the babies terribly."

"I am being selfish," Auriol agreed.

"You are on your wedding trip," she reminded her too. "It will look vastly odd if I remain too long with you on this occasion."

Auriol chuckled and Lady D'Ouro slowed her pace in order to put her hand over her sister-in-law's. "You will soon return to Town, Duchess, and you and I will visit each other frequently, I'm sure."

"Oh yes, I should love that!"

But the Duke, listening in silence said nothing about their return to Town.

Although Auriol genuinely regretted the necessity of Madelaine's return to her home, she also had reservations about being left alone with her husband once again. She could only hope that he would not revert to his mood of cyncism again, for if he did not Auriol felt that their marriage would not be so unbearable after all. Undoubtedly each night she was not averse to his coming to her room, for it was the only time there was any goodwill between them. He knew it and she was in some way angry, both with herself and with him.

On the day after their ride she bade an emotional farewell to her sister-in-law who made her brother promise their parting would be but a short one.

"I shall call on Mrs Ardmore at the first opportunity," she told Auriol as she pulled on her gloves, "and assure her you are in the best of health and spirits."

"She will be delighted to receive you," Auriol answered warmly.

"And I shall request her to have your belongings packed and despatched forthwith." She looked disparagingly at her brother. "Shame on you, Dominic. You really have no notion as to a woman's needs. Three gowns indeed!"

She paused to embrace Auriol and kiss her on the cheek. As she drew away she said softly, looking into Auriol's eyes, "Be patient, my dear, and all will be well."

Before Auriol had a chance to question her on that enigmatic statement she turned to embrace her brother. She smiled brilliantly at him. "You must be kind to her, Dominic, for if you are not you will know my wrath."

She spoke lightheartedly but Auriol suspected a mite of meaning behind her words but the Duke did not take it amiss. He smiled pleasantly at his sister.

"You have no need to fear for the Duchess," he told her. "She is no helpless female. She led me a spritely dance before we were wed so you may do better to admonish her and be kind to me."

"There are some ways in which all women are helpless," she answered soberly before smiling at them both once more and climbing into her carriage.

As the carriage bowled down the driveway, Auriol waved until her arm ached, and when it disappeared from sight her eyes misted with unshed tears.

When she turned away to go back indoors the Duke put one hand on her arm and she was forced to look up at him.

"Tears?" he asked in amazement. "Is it because you will miss my sister's company, or because you have to remain here with me?"

Auriol blinked back her tears then drew herself up proudly. She realised then with a sinking heart her faint hopes had been in vain. There was nothing but mockery in his eyes. He had not reverted to his cruel mockery of her, simply the presence of his sister had kept them apart so she had not noticed it so much of late.

" 'Tis amazing," she said in a husky voice, "we have grown excessively close in the past few days."

He smiled ironically. " 'Tis amazing indeed."

"You are heartless," she accused. "You cannot conceive of what it is to have feelings for anyone other than yourself."

He looked outraged. "This from you, Duchess, who leaves a trail of broken hearts behind?"

Auriol tossed back her curls in a defiant gesture.

"Then be thankful, Your Grace, that you cannot number yourself amongst them."

She lifted her skirts and marched proudly up the steps, leaving him standing in the driveway, roaring with laughter.

XIII

"I must own," said the Duke to Auriol's surprise, "it is pleasant to see the house a hive of activity and to smell beeswax instead of mould everywhere I go."

They were sitting in the drawing room after dinner and Auriol had not seen him since they had bid Lady D'Ouro goodbye earlier in the day.

"It is certainly possible to see an improvement already." She hesitated a moment in her embroidery. "I do hope you will approve my choice of furnishings."

"I am sure I shall," he told her, affecting a yawn. "Your taste has always been exquisite."

"You seem to know a great deal about me, Your Grace, considering the brevity of our association."

"I have known about you far longer than you realise, Duchess. I decided to make you my bride before you were out of the schoolroom so it was incumbent on me to learn as much about you as was possible."

Auriol put her embroidery to one side. "You flatter me."

He smiled slightly, "You need not be. What I learned of your nature did not endear you to me."

Auriol watched him carefully. "But that did not serve to change your mind . . . your intention."

He smiled complacently. "Quite the contrary. I was all the more determined to have you as my wife."

Auriol sprang to her feet. "I cannot understand you!"

"I do not wish you to." He looked at her coldly and it was all she could do not to shiver.

She rushed across to where he was sitting and sank down beside him on the couch. "I cannot pretend to fathom your attitude towards me, but in the past week or so we have not dealt badly together, despite the unfortunate start to our marriage . . ."

Quite unmoved by her agitation and concern he said, "You mean you have not tried to run away from me, but I do not deem to flatter myself on my charm. You simply have not had the opportunity."

Auriol gave a gasp of exasperation. "I do not intend to."

He stared at her coldly. "The fire may be dim but I am quite certain that the spark is not out."

She gave him one of her most appealing looks. She was almost in despair by this time. "Can we not agree to a truce, Dominic? Life could be so much more pleasant, could it not if we were to end this constant state of antagonism?" she ended lamely.

A slow smile spread across his face. "A change of heart, Duchess."

"We must act with reason."

"I am gratified. 'Twas not long ago when you swore to hate me for ever. Did I not say you would change your mind?"

Auriol stiffened. "Do not flatter yourself. I have not changed my mind about my feelings for you. I can have no regard for a man who has treated me as you have done. It simply seems sense that if we are to live together we should try to live in some accord."

He gazed at her, his dark eyes fathomless, and in her confusion her cheeks grew warm and she reached for Suki and cradled her close to her fast beating heart. What she was asking was literally for his consideration of her and a week ago she would rather have died than ask of him anything. Auriol could hardly credit the change in her, a change he was only too well aware of, a change she knew only he could bring about. But she knew she could not continue to live in a constant state of war with him. Life without some vestige of goodwill would not be worth living; she accepted this fact now, for as easily as he could be cruel he could be kind too.

He leaned forward and drew her closer, searching her face carefully. She let Suki go and the spaniel sprang from her lap. Auriol gazed back at him, her heart was beating very fast. She knew this moment was vital to them both. He was divining his own feelings and trying to decide if she was being sincere. Auriol had never been so sincere in her life.

"I'll wager a week ago neither of us expected we would want to," he said softly at last as he drew her against him.

She laid her head on his shoulder and his arms went round her, holding her very close to him. "You do not, I take it, still hunger for Town amusements?" he asked. "Will you be content to remain here with me for the moment?"

She slipped her arms around his neck. " 'Tis impossible to return to Town as yet. I have too much in hand here."

He smiled down at her. She raised her face to his and he was just about to kiss her when there came a knock at the door. They both laughed, happy at their new understanding as they drew apart. Auriol was more than a little gratified that her charm could still work, even on him. There was a time when she had despaired of it.

The Duke got to his feet and Auriol found she was trembling. Their eyes met for a moment and her heart swelled with an emotion she had never before experienced as an understanding passed between them.

Just then a footman came into the room. He was carrying a silver salver and bowed low before them. "Two letters, Your Grace, brought by messenger from London." The Duke frowned and was about to take them from the salver when the footman moved a little to one side, adding, "They are for the Duchess, Your Grace."

The Duke stared at his wife who hardly knew what to say. The footman stood impassively in the centre of the room and Auriol hardly dared to take them from the salver.

It was the Duke who reached over and, taking the letters, dismissed his servant without glancing at the documents at all. He handed them to Auriol who said, smiling faintly, "Ah, this one is from Mama. Will you permit me . . . ?"

"Certainly," he answered and she smiled thanks as she tore open the missive. As she scanned the page he sat down at the other end of the couch and, crossing his legs, he watched her. There was no sound in the room save for the rustle of parchment and although Auriol strove to concentrate on the written word she was very much aware of her husband's attention to her every nuance, even as he took a pinch of snuff.

At last she folded the page and smiled with relief, "All is well, Dominic. She forgives me and welcomes me to her house whenever I choose to visit. The same applies, naturally, to Mr Ardmore."

The Duke looked vaguely bewildered. "Did you doubt that they would, Duchess?"

Auriol blushed and her eyes were downcast. "She must have been exceedingly hurt and bewildered by my thoughtless behaviour."

"The result has been a satisfactory one, so no one need harbour any grudges."

She smiled at him gratefully and without a further word he indicated that she should read the second letter. As she looked down on it the parchment rustled slightly in her hand, for she was trembling all the more now. A sense of foreboding filled her, for she had only to glance at it to recognise the hand. Over the past few months she had received so many passionate notes written in this same familiar hand.

Suddenly she laughed lightheartedly. "Oh, I think I shall read this later. 'Tis of no importance, and it cannot be other than boring for you to have to watch me reading my correspondence."

He waved one languid hand towards her and said before she could secret the document, "Pray, do not mind me, Duchess. The reading of your note will take but a few moments, and you must, I'm persuaded, be anxious to discover who is your correspondent. Be pleased to continue and I will gladly await your attention for a few more moments."

Auriol smiled weakly as he stared at her implacably and with less than steady fingers she had no choice but to break the seal. She scanned the page quickly and her heart sank lower with every word she read. She had written Crispin but a short note and an impersonal one at that; this impassioned epistle was no fitting reply to such an innocent communication.

"Not bad news, I trust," he asked as her face betrayed her dismay. There was a dangerous edge to so polite a voice and she recognised it all too well. Suddenly she was filled with panic, for she felt he already knew who the letter was from, and she saw their newfound accord crumbling into dust.

She stared at him unseeingly and before she could prevent it, he had leaned over and had snatched it from her fingers.

"You have no right to do that!" she protested in anguish. "That letter was addressed to me."

"I have every right, my dear. You are my wife, you recall."

As he began to read the letter Auriol could not bear to watch him and she sprang to her feet, standing with her back towards him. The silence as he read was harrowing and seemed to go on for ever. Every nerve in her body screamed out for him to say something, make some exclamation or remark. Even his sarcasm would have been welcome at that moment.

She did not fear his anger so much as she dreaded

the loss of their newfound accord, so dearly won. Only at that moment did she realise how important it was to her, for a pleasant and considerate husband was quite a different creature to the hard-hearted Duke she had married.

When the paper rustled again she knew he had finished it at last and she swung round on her heel to face him, although it was an effort for her to do so. He raised his eyes from the paper to meet hers. They were very dark and as inscrutable as on the night they had married. She realised, again with wonder, that she never knew what he was thinking; only his implacable and deep-rooted hatred of her. This there was no doubt about.

"Very moving," he said in a cold voice after a moment.

She put out her hands to him in mute appeal. "It is not as you think, Dominic."

"I think you wasted no time in contacting him after you were brought here to be my wife. You have bided your time well, Duchess, in awaiting his reply. No one could have guessed the treachery you were planning behind that winning smile."

"You ill-judge me as always. I merely wrote to tell him I was safe and he need not concern himself for my happiness any longer. I swear it to you, Dominic, that was all I did!"

His lips curved into an ironic smile. "You have no need to take an oath and thus commit a profanity. Do you think I believe a word of yours? I would not believe you if you kissed a dozen bibles and then swore it to me."

Her eyes grew wide with disbelief and when she

could no longer bear to look upon that cold countenance she buried her face in her hands.

"I have tried so hard to make the best of this dreadful marriage I was forced into, so I do not know what I have done to earn such crude scorn from your lips."

"You are who you are," he murmured.

"You talk in riddles!" she cried, and when he appeared totally unmoved by her anguish she sank down into a chair and burst into tears. "I was not to know he would write to me thus, Dominic. You must believe me, for it is the truth."

He picked up the letter again and read it through, seemingly quite unperturbed by his wife's distress. *"Only send me word,"* he quoted, *"and I will come to rescue you from the squalor of your situation, and this time, my dear heart, I will not fail you."*

Auriol's hands dropped from her tear-stained face. "You humiliated him in front of me. Do you not see he wishes to salve his pride a little in my eyes?"

He continued to look at her coldly, as if there had never been anything but hatred between them. "I only wonder what you told him to elicit such an impassioned reply."

"Nothing! Oh, 'twas nothing, Dominic. I made no mention of the misery I did feel at that time. Why will you not believe me?"

The Duke got to his feet and, snatching up the letter again, he crushed it in his hand and flung it into the corner of the room. "It is of no matter now, Duchess," he said in a voice unsteady with anger. "You are *my* wife. I have what I want. He may have you when I do not." He looked at her again. "We return to London tomorrow and he may fawn around your ankles like that spaniel of yours if he has the wish to do so, but I'll wager he will not want you once an unmarried heiress takes his eye."

Auriol shook her head in disbelief. "You are cruel, oh so cruel, Dominic." As he began to prowl the room restlessly, she said, "You know I cannot go to Town just now. There is too much in hand here. I must see the work through to its end now that it is begun."

"You do not need to hang the curtains yourself, Madam. It will be done efficiently in your absence."

"But I want to see everything done myself."

He thumped his hand down on a nearby table so fiercely that a porcelain shepherdess standing on it fell to the floor and was shattered. Immediately the footman came into the room and the Duke shouted, "Leave it!" and the lackey bowed out again.

"Dammit, Madam, you will do as I say or suffer the consequences of being made to."

"You are punishing me," she accused tearfully. "I did not want this role you forced upon me, but now I am reconciled to it you are tearing me away, for you fear I shall receive some satisfaction from it."

He marched towards the door. "I do not wish to discuss the matter any further. You will be ready to travel in the morning. You should be grateful that I send you back to the facile amusements you have always coveted so much."

"And you to Madame Gillray," she said softly.

Her words had the desired effect. He paused and turned to look at her again. "My activities are at no time of any concern to you, Madam, and I ask you not to mention that lady's name again."

"But you will be seeing her, won't you?"

He smiled but there was no mirth in it. "We shall both be seeing our friends shall we not, Duchess?"

He started to go again and she cried, "Dominic, don't go just yet." Her fingers toyed nervously with the pearls at her throat. "Why did you marry me? Oh, I know you needed money to lavish on Hampden Towers . . . and that woman, but there are other women as rich as I and some of them far handsomer, and I know there are many who would receive you gladly. Why did you choose me, Dominic? For you do not even seek to hide your hatred of me. Only tell me what I have done to cause it."

He continued to look at her but said nothing. "Is it because I spurned your advances at some time past? I am sorry, for I truly cannot recall the occasion." She looked at him piteously but no answer was forthcoming. "Oh, please tell me. Did you choose me because you . . . cared for me . . . ?"

An expression of absolute amazement crossed his face and suddenly he began to laugh. Auriol, her nerves already taut, pulled unconsciously at the pearls and the string snapped. The pearls scattered across the floor in every direction. Forgetting the man who was laughing at her so cruelly, Auriol gave a cry of alarm and sank to the floor. She began to gather them together although she could barely see them for the tears that were blinding her eyes.

He came across to her and, pulling her by the arm, he dragged her upright again, and those pearls she had managed to retrieve spilled from her fingers again.

Bewildered and more than a little afraid, she did not resist him as he threw her roughly into a chair and put himself squarely in front of it so that she could not escape.

" 'Pon my soul, Duchess, you believe I harboured some fondness for you. Even now you still have an overweening faith in your own charms."

She looked up at him fearfully. She had seen him angry and she had seen him cold, but never yet had she seen him in such a dangerous mood. He put one hand on each of the arms of the chair and leaned forward so that his face was close to hers. She recalled it was not so many minutes ago that she had thrilled to his closeness where now there was fear.

"If you insist, Duchess, on knowing why I married you, then I shall tell you. Oh, indeed I shall, and I take great satisfaction in doing so, for I have waited for this moment for so many years.

"You were so right in saying I needed money for my estates and you are also right in supposing not any money would do. It was yours I wanted, Duchess, and yours I intended to have."

Auriol continued to look at him in fear. His eyes were one blaze of fury and she could not look away.

"Once Hampden Towers was as grand a house as could be found. It has been in the Seymour family for centuries, and when I was a boy the walls of this decrepit place resounded with the sound of laughter. People were honoured by an invitation to stay at Hampden Towers, to be entertained by the Duke and his wife. Honoured, that is, until my father played a certain game with a certain gentleman and lost all the money he possessed in the world. It has happened before, countless times, and since, for Lady Luck is notoriously fickle with her favours, but Lady Luck was not even allowed at my father's side on this occasion, for the game was a crooked one. The man who won my father's not inconsiderable fortune was a cheat, Duchess, and that man was Richard Stanford."

She clapped one hand to her lips to stifle a cry. "Father? Oh no, you are mistaken. He would never . . . You must be mistaken."

He looked at her triumphantly as he straightened up. "You know, even as you speak, that I am not. I could not be mistaken about so serious a matter as this."

He walked away from her, with all fury gone from his manner. It had been spent in the telling of the tale of a happening that had twisted his true nature into a travesty of what it must once have been. He was well in control of himself now and taking satisfaction in breaking her heart.

"My father knew at last it had been a dishonest game, but he could not prove it; he could only hope to redeem all he had lost by challenging the rogue to a duel, which he did. They met at dawn. My father was by twenty years the older man and not nearly so good a swordsman. Stanford knew this all too well so for once he would fight fairly. He did not kill my father, as well he might, but only injured him sufficiently to ensure no further retribution from that quarter.

"As soon as my father had recovered sufficiently for us to travel we went to France to escape the scandal and to live more cheaply on the bounty of some relatives of my mother. My mother grew old prematurely where once she was as beautiful as you.

"My father was a broken man, both in health and in spirit, and lived for only a few years in his alien environment. My parents, in fact, died within a short time of each other and it was then that I brought my sister home at last.

"During those years of exile I had determined to kill Stanford at the earliest opportunity, but when I returned to England to exact my own retribution I found that someone else had killed him in a duel years before. It seemed my plan for revenge—to recoup the family fortune—was ended, and I grew even more bitter, until it came to my notice he had left a widow, who had remarried and was beyond me, but," he went on, turning to face her again, "there was a daughter, a daughter who had inherited tremendous wealth. My wealth, Duchess."

Auriol choked back a sob. "If it is true 'tis a terrible tale and I pity you most deeply, but it was not my doing, yet you hate me as if it were me."

His eyes gleamed with malice. "Perhaps you are blameless, but there is much of him that I see in you. You have his looks, Duchess," he said softly, "his volatile nature that cares nothing for the feelings of others. I used to watch you preen yourself and take pleasure in breaking the hearts of those bucks who fawned about your feet. You felt no pity, no concern for them, just as your father did not concern himself for those he hurt so unfairly. Revenge would not be half so sweet if you had the looks and nature of that passive mother of yours."

Auriol sprang to her feet. She was beside herself with grief and the tears were coursing down her cheeks unchecked, and she no longer cared if he saw and gloried in her heartbreak. She had done him no injury so the injustice of all he told her was all the more bitter. Iniquity was piled upon injustice.

"Even though I was barely out of the cradle when your misfortune occurred you take delight each and every time you torment me, revenging yourself on me.

"Well, you can pride yourself on your success for you have made my life so miserable I would as lief die tomorrow!"

Unable to see where she was going Auriol almost fell in her effort to escape him. She wrenched open the door, sobbing hysterically as she flew up the stairs, only seeking to put as much space between them as was possible.

XIV

"You cannot possibly travel, ma'am," Hannah told her worriedly as Auriol threshed about in her bed. "You are fevered and it will be the death of you to travel. Let me call a physician and he will tell the Duke so."

"No!" Auriol cried. "I must return to London tomorrow. If I die on the journey the Duke will not care and if I live then at least I can find amusements to divert my mind from this nightmare of my life. Fetch me another cold compress, Hannah," she demanded, throwing aside the one she held to her brow. "I declare my head is on fire."

She had known from the beginning that he had hated her, only she could not in her wildest imaginings begin to conceive of the reason. Now she knew, and the knowledge was well nigh unbearable. Of all the men in England there could be only one who would hate her so implacably and she was married to him.

Those few tender moments when she had believed an understanding possible were gone for ever. The future stretched bleakly ahead and she knew she would have to endure a life of torment and scorn at his hands. He would flaunt his mistress publicly to humiliate her further. She had no doubt of that. And the horror of it all was that he had been planning it for years, whilst she laughed and played, unaware of what was in store for her.

She groaned and Hannah placed the cold compress on her brow. "Now isn't that better, ma'am? Lie still and you will soon feel much much better."

"Never, Hannah. It can never be better. My father was nothing more than a common cheat; a dishonourable man. As long as I live with the Duke he will torment me for it and if I choose to leave him—although if I do I will be alone and penniless in the world—he will tell of it to everyone I know!"

"Now, hush, ma'am. Don't you fret so. It will not seem so bad in the morning."

Auriol gave a broken little laugh. "Do not let yourself fall into the trap laid by males for unwary females to fall into," she told the girl. "Remain heartfree, Hannah, and that will be your salvation."

A faint blush spread up the girl's cheeks. " 'Tis too late for such a warning, ma'am."

Auriol raised herself on one elbow. "Who, Hannah? Who has lulled you into forgetfulness with smooth words you should never believe?"

Hannah stood at the bedside with her eyes downcast. "Bennet, ma'am."

"Bennet! And who may he be?"

"His Grace's valet, ma'am. Surely you remember? Took to each other immediately, we did," she went on eagerly. "Of course, when he brought me here in His Grace's curricle I was suspicious of him, but once everything was made clear we got along fine. With him being His Grace's valet and me being your maid, it seemed an ideal arrangement . . .

"Would you like some broth, ma'am. A tisane perhaps. You have had no supper."

Auriol shook her head and sank back into the pillows again. "You have been betrayed by your own soft heart, Hannah. I was not given a choice, you see. Women of my station cannot remain a spinster, but men are treacherous animals. If you do not need marriage for social or financial reasons you should have no truck with them."

Hannah began to gather up Auriol's roughly discarded clothing, her gown, her petticoats and her stockings. "That would not be natural, ma'am."

"Not natural perhaps, but certainly safer."

As Auriol buried her face in Suki's soft fur Hannah said gently, "Ma'am, I don't know what words have passed between you and His Grace, but I am certain he is fond of you, beggin' your pardon, ma'am."

She looked at Auriol fearfully but her mistress merely smiled tearfully back at her. "You may always speak freely to me, Hannah. You are as loyal a friend as I possess, but I am grieved to tell you that you cannot be more mistaken on this matter, and although you know a considerable amount about my marriage it is more complicated than you know."

"Well, if I *am* permitted to speak freely and that is

only because we are of different stations in life, may I say you and His Grace have not the most stable of temperaments, but angry words are soon forgotten."

Auriol hugged Suki to her. "Would that you are right, Hannah, but this is far more serious than angry words." She stared unseeingly into space. "This, I fear, can never be mended."

XV

The Duke did not come to her room that night. Auriol was not, of course, surprised but she did not know whether she was delighted or disappointed, although she had lain awake for a long time waiting for him. She could only assume their disagreement had reminded him forcibly of her parentage and his disgust of her was too great to overcome now. He had already informed her that Covent Garden lightskirts were as alluring to him and that her fortune was her only attraction for him. He had her fortune and ample opportunity to provoke her misery . . . and for all else he had Madame Gillray.

Auriol had a long, lonely night to think about the long dead father she could not even remember. She had always believed him to be a devil-may-care character, but honourable in spite of all his dissipations. She had cherished romantic thoughts of him throughout her life but now she hated him for this inheritance he had bequeathed to her, and she spent the main part of the night pummelling her pillow in rage and frustration at the cruel blow Fate had dealt her. The Duke's revelations had left her with nothing, not even her pride, and a life that was just an empty shell.

When she gazed at her ravaged face in the mirror the following morning she knew the evidence of her sleepless night was plainly to be seen there.

"He will destroy my looks as well as my soul," she said aloud, and was relieved to have a veiled hat to wear on her journey. Ironically it was the hat she had worn to conceal herself when she had eloped with Crispin. How long ago that seemed, she thought sadly.

She knew then with certainty that she could not spend the rest of her life bound to him by only enmity. Auriol decided at that moment she would escape him in some way before the will to do so left her, before he gave her a child to bind her to him for ever, to use the child as an additional torment against her. She could see that possibility quite plainly and perhaps even now the possibility was a fact.

Even if it were not so and she prayed that it was not, she could see no opportunity of escaping him now, but one was certain to present itself. Auriol's fists clenched on the top of the dressing table in a gesture of defiance. He had not yet killed all the fight in her.

Part Three

*A pity beyond all telling
Is hid in the heart of love.*

I

"He has been back in Town weeks!" exclaimed Madame Gillray. "Weeks, and yet he has not been to see me. Not even a note. *Mon Dieu,* he is a devil that one, to torment so true a heart as this."

The French woman paced the floor of her boudoir restlessly. Not since she had heard news of the Duke's return had she entertained another man. She had waited patiently and with certainty each night for the Duke's arrival, in vain, for incredibly he had not come.

"Perhaps," said Hélène, her personal maidservant and confidante, who was growing accustomed to these lamentations, "the Duke is ill."

"He has never been ill. Besides, he has been seen abroad; at Tattersalls', at Boodles' and at White's. He cannot wait to spend his wife's money."

She glanced at herself in the cheval mirror and then

she leaned closer, seeking lines and creases on that flawless face. Time raced on regardless and Madame Gillray was only too well aware her fortune lie in her looks, and she was not growing younger.

She turned away from the mirror in disgust, and sank down on to a chaise longue, the skirts of her satin gown rustling angrily at the impetuosity of her movements.

"No, it is not he who stays away willingly. It is she who is preventing him coming here. I know it. She has found some way of keeping him with her."

Her eyes narrowed thoughtfully as her fingers toyed nervously with the blue ribbons of her gown. "They have attended balls, routs and assemblies together. Gatherings to which I am excluded."

"He is newly-wed, madame," the woman pointed out. "He may not wish to abandon his wife so soon. After all, appearances must be kept up for a little while."

"Ha! Newly-wed. As if some milk and water miss could keep him from my bed. I don't doubt he feels obliged to introduce her as his wife and the Season is ending so they will be busy. That is why he stays away. He has to act the dutiful husband for a short time. You are right about that, Hélène. I see it now.

"But I cannot help resent it, and resent her. She is his wife only by virtue of her inheritance. I am his true wife; the only one he ever wanted. He would not look at another with love.

"He may have married her for her money but, Hélène, there is something more to it than that and I mean to find out what it is. He was here the night he left for the country, but he said nothing of so urgent a plan to marry. Mr Dainton also left Town at about the same time," she went on, her eyes narrowing thoughtfully, "and appeared some time later badly bruised about the face, but when I spoke to him only the other day, for some reason he was most uncommunicative on the subject, although I admit in my anxiety I may not have approached him in quite the right way. But I will find out the truth of the matter and why my love stays away from me for so long, although from whom I must find out I do not know. I only know that when the Duke spoke of his wife before their marriage there was hatred in his eyes." She looked at her servant. "I mean to get to the bottom of this matter. If she were not there, then he would return to me and it will be as it always was between us. I cannot bear to share him even with a wife he does not love." She stared fiercely into space. "The longer he is away from me, the more I want him."

She jumped to her feet again. "Whatever the cost, Hélène, I mean to have him back!"

II

Once back in London Auriol found that matters were not quite as bad as she had feared.

On their journey from Hampden Towers Auriol was somewhat relieved that the Duke rode on horseback and she was not forced to endure his company more than was absolutely necessary.

She found that the Duke's house in Park Street was far larger than her step-father's house in Mount Street and maintained in a better manner than Hampden Towers. In fact, as she explored it eventually she found it hard to believe the place had belonged to an impoverished nobleman. The Duke had done well in maintaining appearances.

Despite feeling emotionally empty Auriol found, once she had settled in, she was enjoying her role to some degree. As soon as it was known that the Duke and Duchess of Hampden were in Town again not only did callers flock to Park Street, but invitations arrived in handfuls too. All the ambitious Society hostesses were most anxious to be amongst the first to entertain the couple who had made the match of the Season.

Both the Duke and Auriol had an unspoken agreement to appear united before the world, and he dutifully escorted her to the various assemblies although he remained at her side for not a moment longer than was necessary. No one who sighed at this romantic match could have possibly guessed so much hatred lay between them.

And when it came to Auriol returning calls, which she had to force herself to do and appear happy, it gave her a sense of satisfaction to drive out in the Duke's own carriage, emblazoned with his coat of arms. She called as soon as she could on her mother who greeted her joyously, and even her step-father managed to be warm towards her, which indicated that he had already found advantages in being a Duke's father-in-law.

"My child," Mrs Ardmore cried when she saw her daughter and embraced her, "how splendid you look."

Auriol wondered if it were true. Her mother had always tended to believe what suited her but if it were true, it was certainly a tribute to her acting ability.

"Tell me, my dear, was Hampden Towers splendid? I recall it was quite the centre of social activity when I was young."

"It is dilapidated these days, Mama," Auriol answered automatically, "but the Duke has given me instructions to renovate it and the work is in hand already."

Mrs Ardmore clapped her hands in delight. "You will revive the social activity, won't you, Auriol?"

"Not this summer, Mama. There is too much to be done to make the place comfortable for guests. At Hampden House too, I fear, for there is not time to prepare for receptions before the Season ends, but next Season I expect we shall do our share of entertaining."

Auriol almost winced at the thought of the miserable summer between but her mother beamed with pleasure and then she searched her daughter's face carefully before asking, "You are happy, darling, aren't you? I only wish for your happiness."

Auriol could not help but reply acidly, "Providing you are assured of yours, Mama."

Her mother looked troubled and Auriol was immediately contrite. "Of course I am happy, Mama. Who would not be in my position?"

Her mother looked reassured and Auriol thought ironically how easily her mind was settled.

"The Duke wrote to us immediately to tell us you were . . . safe," she laughed nervously. "Such a wonderful man, my dear. Such a wonderful husband, I don't doubt."

Auriol had managed to smile tightly at her mother's praise of the Duke, but once inside her carriage and on the way home her smiles faded and she buried her face in the comfort of Suki's fur and said, "He's a beast really, Suki. Oh, heavens, my love, if only everyone could be like you and love me for myself alone."

As it turned out the Duke did not after all torment her as he had done in the first days of their marriage; that particular pleasure now appeared to have bored him, for now he simply ignored her except when it was necessary to communicate on some small matter in company.

In some ways Auriol hated it more than his continual baiting of her. This mode of living was not natural to either of them, for when he had tormented her she could rise to it at least.

His bedroom was adjoining hers and although she often heard him moving about in there he never came to her. This too relieved her, and yet there were times when she recalled the nights when they were of one accord.

As soon as they took up residence in Park Street, callers began to flock in. Many of her friends, as yet still unmarried, openly envied her situation and the handsome man she had married so romantically without a hint to any of them. It was in a small way balm to the pride he had torn to shreds the night before they left Hampden Towers.

Lady Madelaine D'Ouro was one of her first callers in Park Street, arriving even before Auriol had had a chance to recover from her slight fever brought on by the shock of the Duke's revelations.

Auriol received her in the private sitting room adjacent to her bedroom, and as delighted as she was to see her sister-in-law again she strove to hide the ravages she had experienced at the Duke's hands.

"What delight!" Lady D'Ouro cried. "To have you here in London so soon. That sly brother of mine. I'll wager he knew it all the time."

After embracing her sister-in-law Lady D'Ouro stood back to appraise her the better. "You do indeed look ill, child. If I had known you were so badly in-disposed I would not have intruded so soon."

"Oh, truly, Madelaine, I am so glad to see you."

Auriol was lying on a day bed by the window and her sister-in-law plumped down on the edge of it, dis-placing Suki who slinked off into a corner in disgust.

"Now, tell me, what ails you, my dear?"

"A slight chill only. 'Tis nothing to trouble about," Auriol answered, smiling bravely.

Lady D'Ouro's eyebrows went up a fraction. "Oh, indeed. 'Tis nothing that has put dark rings beneath your eyes." Auriol could no longer meet her bold stare. "And Dominic, is he well?"

"Very well indeed. He has boundless energy and follows every pursuit."

"Is he treating you well, Auriol?" she asked softly and to her surprise Auriol burst into tears.

"Oh, my dear," Lady D'Ouro sympathised, "it is as I suspected; he has ill-used you. I know it."

"He told me his reason for marrying me, Made-laine," Auriol sobbed. "A beating would have been kinder. Physical torture could not be so vile."

Her sister-in-law got to her feet, stiffening with an-ger. Suki surreptitiously slid back into her place next to her mistress.

"What infamy! The toad. How dare he treat you so? Oh, if only he were here at this moment I would box his ears for him."

Auriol laughed hysterically at the thought of it and, ashamed of her outburst, she began to dry her tears.

"Tell me, Madelaine, why is it you do not hate me too?"

Lady D'Ouro walked across to the window and

stared out of it. Auriol noticed now that her pregnancy was becoming noticeable but it in no way diminished her beauty, rather, it enhanced it.

"I did for a while," she said softly, "but when I met you at Hampden Towers I knew I could no longer hate you for something you had no hand in, and I did come to like you for yourself."

She turned her back on the window and smiled at Auriol. "He is as proud as Lucifer, my dear. He harboured his grievance for so long it has become almost a part of him. When we returned to England from France he sat about winning enough money at the gaming tables to provide me with a portion. I tell you, Auriol, when he wants to do something he is a very determined man and no one can deflect him from his purpose."

She frowned. "Is he very cruel, Auriol? He never was before."

Auriol rested her head back on the day bed, for it ached abominably still. Her bronze curls cascaded over it, contrasting markedly with the pale mauve damask upholstery. She sighed deeply as she considered her sister-in-law's question.

"No, he is not cruel at all in the way you are meaning, Madelaine. He is very civil to me now, which is as much as I can hope for, but it is very hard to pay for the sins of another."

Lady D'Ouro let out a little gasp of exasperation and twisted her hands together. "He is a fool. In the past, whatever he had done, I have always been able to credit him with sense, but I see that is sadly lacking of late. Where is he now?"

"I don't know. He never tells me where he is going and I dare not ask.

"He breakfasts in his room so that we need not meet and the only meal we share is dinner, but only if we are to go out afterwards. If we have no evening engagement he dines at his club and does not come home until . . . very late."

"I see you lie awake and notice."

"He is out for so much of the time," Auriol mused. "I suppose he must be with Madame Gillray."

Lady D'Ouro closed her eyes momentarily. "So he told you about her too, did he? I'faith I could murder him."

Auriol could not help but laugh again. "He did not need to tell me. Everyone knows about Madame Gillray and the Duke."

Lady D'Ouro smiled gently. "She is a very beautiful and experienced woman, and he has known her a great many years."

"I knew of their association before we were married. It is not unusual in our circles, Madelaine."

"I am grateful to say that I am not in a position to have to accept it." Lady D'Ouro shook her head then. "And you accept the Duke's behaviour so much more readily than I could ever have believed."

"I am not the woman I was, Madelaine," she answered, staring blankly into space. "I don't care what he does."

Her sister-in-law turned away again. "You disappoint me. I should not have thought even Dominic could rob you of your spirit."

Auriol put one hand to her head and sighed. "He

does not plague me, I have a great social position and I am respected by all. It must be enough.

"It makes no matter what I do or say; the Duke will still do as he pleases and making scenes will not improve my position. Nothing can be changed by anything I do or say."

"Well, I cannot accept such nonsense," she said irritably. "Dominic made my own happy marriage possible. I married with pride the man I loved because he provided me with a portion I would not have otherwise had. I want him to achieve such happiness too but it is impossible whilst his heart is filled with hatred. I just cannot sit back and watch you both growing more bitter. I must have words with my brother."

Auriol swung her legs over the side of the day bed. "Oh, do not, I beg of you, Madelaine. If you know the Duke at all you will realise it will be to no avail.

"We live as strangers, but it is not an unbearable existence. The Duke does not demur in accompanying me in our circle, to every assembly to which we are invited. No one aside from our own three selves know of his real reasons for marrying me, so I am able to hold up my head in company and retain some last shreds of my pride. As long as I am able to do that I shall be satisfied, but if you or I displease him, Madelaine, he may not keep up that facade and I will be shamed before everyone. Only if my father's shame is not known to the world can I be content!"

Lady D'Ouro sank down beside her sister-in-law and gathered up her hands in her own. "Oh, my dear, what can I do to help, then?"

"Nothing, nothing at all," Auriol cried in despair. "If you will, please be my friend, that is all I ask of you, but as to the other, no one can do anything to help!"

III

Lady D'Ouro was in some mood of indignation when she returned home a short while later. She was a woman who, although possessing her fair share of the Seymour volatile nature, also had little time for fools, and her brother, she considered, was a fool. She had been at home for only a few minutes, only long enough to remove her hat and gloves when a footman presented her with a calling card.

Lady D'Ouro frowned at it. "What on earth can *she* want with me?" she murmured thoughtfully. She had intended visiting the nursery immediately on her return and was about to instruct the lackey to convey her apologies to her caller when she changed her mind.

"Very well, Fowler, show the lady up immediately," adding to herself when he had gone, "I cannot do anything to help Auriol and that idiot husband of hers if I ignore his *chère amie*, so perhaps my receiving her may achieve something, although," she sighed, "I cannot conceive what it could be."

Moments later Lady D'Ouro received her visitor with more cordiality than she harboured towards the woman, but she was by far too shrewd to greet her brother's mistress with too much warmth, so she retained a certain degree of condescension in her manner.

Marie Gillray, Lady D'Ouro could not help observe, was looking uncommonly handsome even though her age could not fall far short of forty. She breezed into the drawing room wearing a rose pink walking gown of crushed velvet with a matching hat adorned with pink feathers atop a confusion of blonde curls. There were few women who could rival Marie Gillray in looks, and it amazed Lady D'Ouro that for all his fine looks the Duke had managed to remain favourite for so long, for there was many a titled man with fortune who vied for her favour.

The civilities were exchanged briefly and Lady D'Ouro invited her unwanted guest to sit down on a couch opposite to her seat. She said nothing once the initial greetings were done with and waited patiently for Madame Gillray to speak.

At last the Frenchwoman realised that Lady D'Ouro was not going to make her task an easy one, which she should have guessed, for this lady was no more a fool than was her brother. She glanced around briefly and then turned her dazzling smile on the younger woman.

"What a pleasant room this is, Lady D'Ouro. So light and airy."

Lady D'Ouro forced herself to smile back at Madame Gillray although she was sorely tempted to box her ears for her impudence in assuming the manners of a great lady. Oh, Dominic, she fumed silently, you have a lot to answer for if you cannot distinguish a real lady from a sham.

"I fancy you have seen it before."

"Not as often as I would like, Lady D'Ouro. It seems a great time since we last met, and this thought prompted me to make good this omission. I trust you and Sir Donald are keeping in good health."

"Oh very," Lady D'Ouro answered, wondering how soon she could rid herself of this woman's presence.

Marie Gillray beamed. "And the dear children? So sweet. They must be growing very fast, as amazingly children always seem to do." She laughed delicately. "One day they are but babies and seemingly only the next they are young men and women."

"They are well too." Lady D'Ouro hesitated and then she smiled sweetly. "I had no idea you were so fond of children, Madame."

"Oh, indeed I am." She sighed. "I am very fond of them. It is to my great sorrow that poor Gillray did not live long enough to honour me with them."

There was a further silence between them and then Marie Gillray said, "Your brother, Lady D'Ouro, is very fond of his nephew and his nieces . . . He talks of them often to me. I feel I know you all so well, almost as if I were a part of the family, in fact."

Madelaine D'Ouro settled back more comfortably in her seat. "The Duke has always been fond of children, Madame Gillray. Needless to say he hopes that he and the Duchess will be blessed with them before too long a time has passed."

The smile remained on the woman's face. "Oh, indeed it would be a great pity if the title were to die out because of the lack of an heir, which happens so sadly on too many occasions. The Duke is very much aware of his obligations in this matter. The Duchess is," she ventured, "in good health."

"Excellent," Lady D'Ouro answered coldly.

"Such a pretty child," murmured the Frenchwoman and Lady D'Ouro did not miss the note of sourness in her voice.

And almost young enough to be your daughter, Lady D'Ouro thought to herself, and then, leaning forward slightly, she said, "She was pretty, Madame Gillray, but since her marriage to the Duke, strange to tell she has become in truth a great beauty. 'Tis only happiness that brings about such a bloom as the Duchess bears upon her cheeks." She put one hand to her breast. "As his only other kinswoman, Madame Gillray, I have often grieved for his loneliness, which I knew to be very profound despite the great number of his acquaintances. The delight he took in my own family only served to underline that, but now it does my heart good to see him with his bride."

The smile froze on Madame Gillray's face to the great satisfaction of Lady D'Ouro. It made those few falsehoods worthwhile, although when she recalled her visit to Hampden Towers it was not so far removed from the truth. Madelaine D'Ouro had a shrewd idea that Auriol had been very close to melting her brother's hard heart.

"Come now," Marie said in a quiet voice, slightly

thick to one who was seeking satisfaction from her chagrin, "I also know him well. I can boast of knowing the Duke very well indeed, as you are aware, Lady D'Ouro; better than any other woman alive, if I may say so, and this marriage of his is no love-match. 'Tis only a marriage of convenience."

Lady D'Ouro sat up straight. "Who dares to say so?"

The Frenchwoman was now fully in control of the situation and she smiled in apparent wonderment. "Why, Lady D'Ouro, your brother, of course." She leaned forward eagerly now, seizing metaphorically the bit between her teeth. "Do not look so shocked, my lady; there are no secrets between a man and a woman who are as close as the Duke and I have been these several years. He made the situation abundantly clear to me the very night before he wed."

The other woman almost choked in her vexation and could not hide it. She jumped to her feet, for in her outrage she could no longer remain seated. "Oh, shame on him!"

Lady D'Ouro was angry enough that the Duke had so cruelly informed his wife of his reason for marrying her, thus shattering the poor child's sensibilities, but to tell his mistress and to shame Auriol the more . . . Madelaine D'Ouro's rage knew no bounds.

"Such marriages are most commonplace," Marie Gillray pointed out complacently. "The Duchess will in due course follow her own heart as does the Duke."

The other woman sighed, realising that this was inevitably true, and the Frenchwoman pressed on, sensing victory now. "Of course I am well aware that this is no mere marriage of convenience in the usual sense . . ." Lady D'Ouro swung round to stare at her. "I hope the Duke is not acting as vindictively as he intended towards the poor child."

Lady D'Ouro clenched her hands together in fury. "I do declare I *will* kill him. To tell you of his cold-blooded plan for revenge goes beyond all that is bearable."

Marie Gillray laughed. "I am sure you will not do anything against the Duke. Please be assured, my dear Lady D'Ouro, I am most discreet where your dear brother is concerned, for he is so close to my heart. He is the most . . . impassioned of men and therefore I am persuaded that the matter was not as serious as he made out to me . . ."

Lady D'Ouro prowled restlessly around the room. She had all but forgotten who her visitor was, so great was her fury. Her anger was most certainly directed towards the Duke, her brother, but she felt considerable chagrin that this strumpet should know the family's most intimate secret.

"Oh, it was serious enough," she answered, wishing she had her brother in the room at that moment. "The Duchess's father was indeed a cheat and the cause of all our misfortunes at that time, but it was my father's fault too in gambling so deep. It was not the first time it had happened . . ."

Marie Gillray smiled with satisfaction and, drawing a sigh, she sank back into the cushions of the couch and attended sympathetically as the Seymour temper swept away all Madelaine D'Ouro's restraint and regard for all else.

IV

Auriol's feet ached almost as much as her heart had done since leaving Hampden Towers. The Duchess of Devonshire's masked ball was one of the last big assemblies of the Season and a magnificent affair as were all those at Devonshire House.

The great house was ablaze with lights, and music poured from every room. Auriol felt as if she might suffocate beneath her mask and domino, and could hardly wait for the time when she could remove them both. The jewels worn by the female guests glittered in the candlelight, providing in themselves enough light by which to see. Auriol was ironically aware that this masquerade could be symbolic of her life, for her mode of living now was no more than that.

Her smile had always been a ready one, but now she found she had to force it to make certain no one guessed that all was not well. There were couples present tonight with just such disagreeable marriages but her pride forbore her from admitting hers was one of them, and she wanted no one's pity although she sensed from some of the looks given her there were those who already did so.

Auriol dreaded the imminent ending of the Season, when all the great families moved to their country estates. With all the social activity of late she had not been forced to face her husband and to be alone with him for any length of time. She could hardly bear to contemplate a return to Hampden Towers with matters so strained between them, and she could only hope that Madelaine and her family would want to accompany them.

As she danced a minuet with someone she could not identify, although he had seemed vaguely familiar to her, she searched the crowd for sight of the Duke. He had dutifully escorted her to the ball but had left her side almost immediately the dancing began. Auriol had not been left without a partner for the entire evening but it was humiliating for her husband not to be numbered amongst them, for at least one occasion.

She caught sight of him as the dance ended; he had been partnering the Duchess of Devonshire herself and just now the great lady was laughing at something he had said to her. He can be so charming, Auriol thought, and yet there was another side to his nature that few other people saw.

She considered the Duchess for a moment or two. She was not exactly a beauty but she had an abundance of wit and charm which attracted people of both sexes to her like moths to a candle. Auriol knew that as the Duchess of Hampden she too could hold an enviable

position as leader of Fashionable Society if she so
wished, only she had not the heart.

Reluctantly as the minuet finished she drew her attention to her partner who had danced so well at her
side. The dance had ended but he showed no eagerness to relinquish her hand. She smiled shyly and attempted to lead him from the floor, for she had no
desire to dance again with this man. Indeed, she
would be thankful not to have to dance at all although
the night was yet young. There was no chance of escape yet.

"Auriol," the man said in a whisper as she turned
to go. "Do you not know who I am?"

Auriol immediately stopped in the centre of the
dance floor and whirled round on him. "Crispin," she
gasped.

The colour drained from her cheeks and she felt
suddenly weak. Automatically she raked the crowd
with her eyes for sight of the Duke but to her relief he
was nowhere to be seen.

"I must speak with you in private," he said in a
voice that was low and urgent.

Auriol tried to extricate her hand from his but
failed to do so. "I cannot. The Duke . . ."

Auriol fancied that he smiled behind his mask.
"Your husband has just gone into the card room and
as he has not troubled you all evening, I fancy he will
not do so now."

"But it will soon be time to unmask and we will
both be seen quite plainly."

He drew her towards one of the windows. "Then
before we are forced to do so it is the best time to
talk."

She allowed him to lead her unprotesting from the gathering. She was torn between the desire for his company and the fear of her husband seeing them together. Whilst still masked it was certain no one else would recognise them at least.

Outside the air was refreshing and Auriol took a deep, welcome breath of it, for the vast ballroom had been stifling. They paused only momentarily before he drew her further into the shrubbery, where the way was lit by lanterns and masked revellers, some of them the worse for drink, ran laughing between the trees and bushes.

"Oh, Crispin," she said when the sound of revelry was fainter, "I have been so concerned for you. Were you hurt very badly?"

"My bodily bruises have healed," he said meaningfully.

"The Duke said you would recover with no ill-effect, but he would not allow me to stay to attend you at the inn, although I begged of him to allow me to do so. He said he would hurt you more if I did not go with him."

"I did not believe you had gone willingly." Auriol turned away in distress. At least with this man she need not pretend that all was well.

He took her arm and drew her close again. "I meant every word I wrote in that letter, Auriol. I can hardly bear to think of what your life must be like with him. If there is any way out of this preposterous marriage . . ."

"No, there is not!"

"Mark me well. He took me unawares the once but I will not fail you a second time. Since my return to

London I have spent much time learning the art of fisticuffs and my swordplay would not shame the Duke himself."

"You will not challenge him!" she cried, aghast.

"Only if you wish it, my love."

Auriol buried her head in her hands. "Oh, no, Crispin. I could not bear bloodshed. He can still kill you. He practises with a fencing master every day he is in Town, and he is so good at it."

"Perhaps so. Perhaps the married happiness we planned together cannot now be and I needs must seek a wife elsewhere." His voice was low and urgent now.

Auriol raised her head proudly and choked back her tears. "Of course and I wish you happy in your choice."

He shook his head impatiently. "Only hear me out, Auriol. That would only be an expedient; you must surely realise that. It is you I really want and always have done, but even now there is no reason why we cannot find a little happiness together. It is quite accepted, my dear. Allow me to call upon you when the Duke is . . . when he is not at home."

She turned away in confusion. Of course it was accepted. There were few enough married women who did not have their gallants. It would be better than this sterile life she was leading. Crispin would love her devotedly—she did not doubt that—and bring some happiness into her life. It was a reassurance she desperately needed.

"What do you say, my love?"

"I don't know, Crispin. I must consider it. I always

intended to marry a man I loved, so I never thought I would come to seek a gallant."

"It won't be in the same way as others, Auriol. We, at least, love each other.

"The Duke has your fortune which is all he wanted from you. He will not care."

"No, he will not care," she echoed in a whisper.

"And he does have his own amusement."

Auriol looked at him then. "I do not wish to be an amusement."

He laughed softly. "*You* will not be, my love. I do love you, Auriol."

She was moved almost to tears by his declaration. "It is so much less than we wanted."

"It is as much as we can hope for."

The air was suddenly rent with whoops and cracks that heralded the start of the fireworks display which illuminated the sky, and Auriol started uneasily. They were alone in the garden now as everyone had gone to watch the display and to unmask.

"It is time to unmask," he reminded her.

Auriol fumbled with the ribbons of her mask and drew off her domino. "What relief. These masquerades are vastly tedious. If it were not held by the Duchess of Devonshire herself, I would not have come."

"In that case we would not have had this chance to be together."

"There would have been others, Crispin, as there will be in the future. At least there are bound to be times like these."

" 'Tis not enough," he said heatedly. "And if you will only own to it, you know that too."

He too took off his mask and they stood gazing at

each other. It was the first time she had seen him since her marriage and now she looked at him with new eyes. He was still as fair and as handsome as ever, his eyes were still that startling blue, but he looked so much younger than she remembered.

"Only say the word, Auriol," he murmured, close to her ear.

She was startled out of her thoughts and she looked away in confusion. "Let me consider it a while, Crispin. My situation is still so new."

"But none the less miserable."

She turned quickly. "I must return before I am missed. The Duke for all his uncaring ways acts strangely when you are around, and I wish to avoid as much unpleasantness as is possible."

They walked slowly back to the house just as the last rocket faded and died in the sky. The terrace from which the best view could be obtained was fast emptying now as new amusements beckoned, and by the time Auriol and Crispin reached it the only person still remaining was the Duke himself.

Auriol automatically drew back slightly, but he saw them immediately and there was no escape. Auriol held her breath for a moment, but then breathed again as her husband bowed coldly to the other man before saying, "Ah, Duchess, I was looking for you. 'Tis time to be gone."

On any other occasion she would have objected to leaving so early but this time she was so grateful to avoid an unpleasant scene she acquiesced easily, murmuring only, "Goodnight," to Mr Dainton.

There was, she fancied, an uncomfortable silence between them as they rode through the streets of Mayfair on their way home to Park Street. Auriol had placed herself in one corner of the carriage in order to put between them as much room as possible, which was an unavailing gesture as it was only a matter of a few inches more than usual. Covertly she watched him take a pinch of snuff. He was entirely relaxed and she marvelled at his ease.

" 'Twas an exceedingly good rout," she said when the silence was well nigh unbearable.

"I am glad you enjoyed it my dear," he answered mildly.

Auriol drew a sigh of relief. She allowed herself a glance at him and he was gazing at her. His head rested on the back of the seat and his eyes were half closed as they surveyed her. She was suddenly uneasy again, for she distrusted the very ease of his manner; there was an ironic curl to his lip.

"I would be an unnatural creature if I did not enjoy one of Her Grace's routs," she said in a high bright voice.

"And the sight of Mr Dainton so well recovered no doubt sent your spirits soaring far more than any other entertainment provided by Her Grace."

Her heart sank. She wished now she had borne the silence. "I am . . . always glad to see a friend in good health."

"But he is not so good a friend as he was, Duchess . . . now that you are no longer the prospect of good fortune that you were a short time ago."

"You attribute everyone with your own base instincts, Your Grace. Some people have true feelings for others."

"I doubt if Mr Dainton can be numbered amongst

them," he said lightly. "You will find his interest in you will wane now."

She rounded on him angrily. "There you are wrong, Mr Dainton is as in love with me as ever."

One eyebrow went up a shade. "So he has already applied for the position of gallant, has he? 'Twas to be expected. You would keep him well provided with cash."

Auriol felt confused. "You do not object?"

The Duke yawned delicately. "My dear, you may conduct your affairs as you wish, provided you have a care for the name you now bear."

The carriage drew to a standstill outside the house in Park Street. A footman waited for them to climb down but Auriol simply stared at her husband coldly.

"I shall certainly conduct myself with propriety, Your Grace, as I know you will do, and when I am thus engaged you will be free to follow your own inclination."

He laughed. "I do not need you to grant me freedom to do that. I shall always follow my inclination."

She looked away from him. Now he had approved her taking a lover she felt more miserable than if he had displayed anger.

"You may climb down, my dear," he said leaning forward now.

"Are you coming inside?" she asked in surprise.

"The night is young, and so am I," he said, flourishing his hand dramatically.

Auriol stiffened. "You are going to that . . ." Words failed her.

He merely smiled. "You refer, I believe, to Madame Gillray." Auriol could not meet his eye.

"She is old. I cannot imagine why you condescend to visit her still."

"Oh, come now, Duchess, you are too harsh in your judgement of the lady. She is you must know, a most beautiful, witty and accomplished woman, and age can only mellow her attraction."

"And her father was not a cheat," she said bitterly and met his confused gaze again. Her eyes flashed with anger. "Well I doubt if she ever had one! But that is of no account to you, I dare say."

"Precisely. Be pleased to step down, Duchess; I am anxious to be gone."

Auriol waited no longer. She stepped down from the carriage and without so much as glancing back she marched proudly into the house so that he could not see her tears of anger.

The Duke watched her go before sinking back into his seat, closing his eyes momentarily and then saying wearily to his driver, "Take me to Boodles . . ."

V

Marie Gillray sat before her dressing mirror, draped from neck to ankles in a plain silk powdering robe. She leaned forward and peered into the mirror and found nothing she saw there to her satisfaction as she pulled and prodded at her skin, noting every sign of imminent decay.

She nodded presently for her hairdresser to commence his work and looked into the mirror to the reflection of the man who was sitting behind her on a silk padded day bed. He was wearing evening dress and was, perhaps, attired a little more colourfully than good taste now dictated.

He sat on the edge of the seat, appearing a little bewildered at the honour bestowed upon him, and rather selfconscious at being for the first time in the perfumed boudoir of the infamous Frenchwoman.

As the hairdresser began to busy himself Marie

Gillray said to her guest, "Mr Dainton, you must decide for me what I shall wear tonight."

Crispin Dainton sat up straight with some difficulty, for Marie Gillray's furniture did not make it easy to do other than recline. "I, *Madame*? I cannot decide what is fitting for one such as you."

Madame Gillray bit back her irritation at having to invite such a dull and gauche young man to her inner sanctum, and smiled sweetly.

"Nonsense, my dear. You have, I have always noted, had the most exquisite taste. You surely will not disappoint me tonight."

Crispin Dainton was more than a little flattered. Invitations to the *demi-rep's* house were not commonplace and in the past she had barely acknowledged his existence. His disastrous encounter with the Duke of Hampden, although it was now some weeks past, still stung his pride and this sudden elevation in his fortunes was most opportune.

Marie Gillray nodded to her maid who commenced to bring forward a dazzling array of gowns for his perusal. The task seemed a daunting one, for each gown was more magnificent than the rest. No sooner had he decided upon one than the abigail brought forth another.

"Well, Mr Dainton, which do you choose? Which will become me best, do you think?"

"A sack would become you, *Madame*," he answered, sitting back comfortably and crossing his legs.

Marie Gillray dimpled. "Oh, you dear boy. You are so sweet."

Feeling more confident of his charms now he went

on, waving his arm languidly, "The violet taffeta, *Madame*, for your eyes are more violet than blue."

Marie Gillray clapped her hands in delight. "And so it shall be, Mr Dainton." She looked at her hairdresser who was poised for work. "Well, Ferdinand, you have heard Mr Dainton's choice of gown, what do you suggest now?"

The hairdresser looked pensive for a moment and then sketched a vague design in the air above her head. "Matching feathers—five of them—gilt leaves, and plums. We shall make an exquisite creation."

"Plums?" echoed the Frenchwoman.

"Oh, yes, *Madame*," the hairdresser assured her. "You will create quite a fashion. Vegetables and flowers are quite *outré*."

She peered at her maid who was packing away the discarded gowns. "Hélène, be pleased to fetch some plums."

The abigail hurried to do her mistress's bidding whilst Marie Gillray settled back to allow the hairdresser to grease, powder and pad her hair.

"Come along over here, Mr Dainton," she cooed.

Crispin Dainton also hurried to do her bidding. She pushed her patch box towards him, ordering him to "Choose."

After moment's hesitation he selected three and was about to return to his seat when she said sweetly, "But where do you suggest they go, Mr Dainton?"

He looked a little taken aback and then indicated, "Here, here and here, *Madame*."

"I am not quite sure . . ."

To his acute discomfort he was forced close to her to show her physically just where the patches should be placed. Her perfume, her womanliness was almost overpowering.

"Ah, now I understand," she beamed at him. "Thank you so much, Mr Dainton."

"Fortune has not favoured your love life well of late," she said as he seated himself again.

He looked startled; this coming so soon after such close contact with her. "I beg your pardon, *Madame*?"

"You were thwarted in your efforts to marry a certain lady who has been elevated quite recently and unexpectedly to the aristocracy."

Crispin Dainton looked distinctly vexed. "So you know of that," he said crossly. "The Duke, I suppose . . ."

Marie Gillray smiled with satisfaction. "I know everything, *chéri*. I am quite *au fait* with the whole business."

Hélène returned with the plums and after handing them to Ferdinand went about her work again.

"I will speak plain with you, Mr Dainton," said the woman. "I never sought for such an elevated place in life but despite that, this match does not suit me well."

"Nor me, *Madame*," murmured the young man.

"You are still fond of the Duchess?"

"I am devoted to her," he said dully, reminding herself for the countless time of how nearly was her fortune his.

"You know, Mr Dainton, if you are clever about this she can still be yours."

"I am aware of it, *Madame*. Her marriage as you must know is not a happy one and she receives me as well as she has always done."

"It is more unhappy than you know. She needs your

help desperately, Mr Dainton. Devoted as I am to the Duke I cannot stand by and allow him to destroy her, as he plans to do."

Crispin Dainton's eyes opened wide, "You exaggerate, *Madame*."

"No, *certainement*."

"Please keep your head still, *Madame*," begged the hairdresser.

"He is intent on destroying her," she went on undaunted. "He can be a fiend as I know only too well, but I am more of a match for him than that poor child."

She lowered her voice. "I will tell you why, Mr Dainton . . ." and she commenced to tell him the story that Lady D'Ouro had inadvertently revealed.

"But that is terrible," he cried when Marie Gillray had finished. "It is the most infamous thing I have ever heard."

"My sentiments entirely, Mr Dainton."

"He cannot blame poor Auriol for the wrong her father did."

"He was mad with grief for what happened, and harboured his hatred for years, only waiting for the day he could exact retribution, only he cannot punish Mr Stanford, and you must admit, *chèri*, Miss Stanford has not always endeared herself to everyone."

"Some insolent puppies have presumed too much," he protested, "and incurred her wrath. No one, not even the sweetest natured person, could tolerate such presumption."

"And let it not be said that Miss Stanford is *that!*" Madame Gillray said with a gay laugh.

"She is an angel!" He looked appealingly at the Frenchwoman. "What can I do to stop him?"

"He took her from you," she reminded him. "You could now redress yourself by taking her from him, and also save Her Grace from his wickedness and cruelty."

He sprang to his feet. "He shall meet me over this."

Marie Gillray put one hand out placatingly. "No, *mon chéri*, that is not the way to help the Duchess, or indeed, yourself. There is, however, another way." She paused momentarily. "Would you still elope with her?"

Crispin Dainton sank down into his seat again and put his chin in his hand. "That is impossible. I have no money and neither has she."

"That is where you are wrong, Mr Dainton. True her inherited fortune is lost to you both should she leave the Duke, but the Duchess possesses a fortune in jewels which can be packed into a small box. If you flee to the continent—and I will give you addresses— you will be able to live in splendid comfort for the rest of your lives!"

Crispin Dainton's eyes grew bright at the thought. Auriol's jewels were certainly magnificent. "The packet leaves Folkestone tomorrow morning," the woman told him. "You both could be on it and on your way to a new life as soon as tomorrow!"

Just as suddenly his enthusiasm waned. "I have no ready money to see us on our way, *Madame*. The duns have been hounding me for months. I can get no credit anywhere."

"Oh, never fear on that score, Mr Dainton. As your dear friend I can do no less than make you a loan—which," she added quickly, "you can repay as soon as you are able."

"Tomorrow," he echoed bleakly. " 'Tis too soon."

"Do you wish the Duchess to endure more misery at his hand. If you delay in order to plan this more finely there will be no advantage. She has no guile, *chéri*, the Duke will become suspicious and she will reveal all if you delay. All will be lost."

"But I need time to persuade her . . ." he protested. "I shall have no opportunity to see her."

"You are so faint-hearted, Mr Dainton. Such obstacles are of no account.

"You are to accompany me to Ranelagh tonight, are you not?"

"It is my honour to do so, *Madame*."

"Well, they are certain to be there tonight. All the *beau monde* will be there."

"Including the Duke, her husband," Mr Dainton said sourly.

"Let me attend to the Duke, Mr Dainton. You shall have your opportunity to speak with his wife for as long as you wish; I assure you of that. Later too, let me tell you. He will still be . . ." she laughed "occupied when the boat sails to take you and her to a new life of love . . . and luxury, and all your troubles will be over."

"If only we could do it," he breathed. "To save her from such a fiendish plan! From that devil!"

"She will be eternally grateful to you. You will have, in effect, *mon ami*, saved her life, for I am told she already grows haggard."

Crispin Dainton's eyes narrowed thoughtfully.

"And you will ensure there is no interference from the Duke?"

She laughed delightedly. "I assure you he will not even know of it until you are safely across the Channel." The hairdresser removed the gown and Madame Gillray, after surveying herself with satisfaction, stood up. She flashed Crispin a brilliant smile. "All I have to do now is put on my gown and we shall be ready to depart! In less than an hour, Mr Dainton, you will be with your heart's love!"

VI

The atmosphere at Ranelagh was very gay. Gorgeously gowned ladies wandered down the walks beneath arbours with their beaux, and the scent of apple blossom and the sound of music drifting was everywhere in the air.

Within the magnificent rotunda a box was reserved for the Duke of Hampden's party and within it the conversation was excited, but Auriol could not respond to the festive air. She was miserable, although she did not know why. Matters were far more satisfactory than the first few days of her marriage had led her to expect, and yet she was more unhappy now than she had been then.

Young Lord Nunwich, who had been at her side almost constantly for the past few days, attempted to feed her some tit-bits from the cold collation set out before them. Auriol merely refused them with a wan smile that caught at the young man's heart.

She kept on recalling her conversation with Crispin and his avowal of devotion to her. She had wanted him as her husband, but did she, she wondered, want him as a lover? In truth she no longer knew what she wanted. Her relationship with men invariably led her to grief. She wished she could decide to dispense with them entirely, but her first few days of marriage had awoken in her a new awareness of life that even her deepest misery could not diminish.

Hampden was sitting close to her but as always he practically ignored her the entire time. With so many people of their acquaintance promenading in the rotunda and pausing to speak, it was not surprising that husband and wife did not have an opportunity to converse. Indeed, it was not customary. But Auriol knew that this was not the reason for his indifference and it hurt.

He was in conversation with Sir Donald D'Ouro, his brother-in-law, one of the members of their party that evening. "Pregnancy makes Madelaine peevish," she heard him say, "she has scarce exchanged a civil word with me in days."

"That is most unlike my wife," her husband answered gravely. "I will have words with her."

"I beg you do not, Donald. She will recover her spirits in good time, I don't doubt."

"The Duchess looks pale, Hampden, this past se'night. Many have commented on it. Do we dare to hope . . . ?"

Auriol's cheeks grew pink. Despite her jumbled thoughts on the subject she had harboured some hopes too, but she knew now that there was none, for too long had passed since they left Hampden Towers.

The Duke laughed harshly at his brother-in-law's tentative question. "I think not, Donald."

A few moments later he looked at his wife and she quailed. "Duchess, you are picking at your food. Poor Lord Nunwich looks most distressed. Can *I* not tempt you with some mutton?"

"I am not hungry," she answered in a soft voice.

"Come now," he coaxed, "you must eat or you will grow thin, and I cannot abide skinny females."

Auriol made a gasp of exasperation and was thankfully diverted by Lord Nunwich whom she attended with far more interest than she would normally. A few moments later a lackey appeared with a note for the Duke who glanced at it, swore roundly and got to his feet.

"You will excuse me," he said to the party in general and Auriol watched him leave, wondering what or whom had called him away.

"Would you like to walk, Your Grace?"

Auriol looked at the young man blankly for a moment or two, and then said, "Yes, yes, I would, for the atmosphere grows oppressive."

She smiled at Lady D'Ouro who frowned as she watched her go. Auriol was glad she had moved from the box. Walking beneath the fragrant arbours in the semi-darkness she felt almost anonymous; less like the Duchess of Hampden and more like some ordinary creature with no cares to weigh her down. Shadowy figures beneath trees and arbours took advantage of the cloak of night to embrace in anonymity. Auriol as she saw them felt quite empty inside. There were so many men who would be willing to become her lover, men of status, wealth and good looks, but in truth she had to admit she did not want any of them now.

She conversed with her escort, but in reality she had no idea about what they spoke, for her mind was constantly engaged in her own misery. Suddenly a figure emerged from the shrubbery and Auriol recognised him at once.

"Madam, may I speak with you?" Crispin asked, glancing uncertainly towards her escort.

Auriol was at first uncertain too and then she turned to Lord Nunwich. "Please excuse us, my lord. I shall rejoin you presently."

The young man was obviously not pleased to relinquish her company, but he had no choice but to acquiesce. He bowed stiffly and withdrew.

"I did not look to see you again so soon," she said in her delight at his appearance.

"Your warmth gratifies me, Auriol, or is it simply that Nunwich bores you?"

She dimpled. "He does at times, but that is not why I was so pleased to see you."

He took her hand and led her towards the canal. She hesitated fractionally but he said, "Have no fear, my darling, the Duke is occupied with Madame Gillray." She let out a little involuntary cry. "I have seen them together not minutes ago. They will no doubt be engaged for some time."

After they had walked in silence for a while Crispin stopped and looked at her. "You look drawn, Auriol. Are you not well?"

Her hand went automatically to her face. "I . . ."

"Do not seek to explain, my love, for I know it all,

the misery you endure so bravely and I have the answer to our problems. You shall not remain beneath his roof another night."

Auriol drew back in astonishment. "What do you mean, Crispin?"

"We are to leave for France tonight, you and I!"

His eyes gleamed with excitement and she laughed at so ridiculous an idea. "We cannot. I cannot! This is sheer madness."

"You must."

She laughed again. "Shall we fly like birds, Crispin? From here? Now?"

"Do not make jest," he said earnestly.

"Then you should not make jest also."

"He means to ruin you, Auriol; ruin your health and your spirit. I know it all, you see, his plan for revenge, his reason for marrying you."

She drew further from him, shaking her head in disbelief. "You *know* about it. How do you know, Crispin?"

His lips twisted into a smile of derision. "His mistress told me. She knows every detail."

Auriol's eyes opened wide in horror and her hands flew to her lips to suppress a cry. "Madame Gillray told you! He told *her* about my shame . . ."

" 'Tis not your shame, Auriol. 'Pon my soul, he has you believing it too."

"Oh, I cannot bear it, Crispin! If Madame Gillray knows and has told you, everyone will know."

"The shame will be *his* if it is seen you had to run away to escape his cruelty."

She buried her face in her hands and swayed back

and forth on her heels. "I cannot bear the shame, Crispin."

"You don't have to, my love. Only listen to me. The packet leaves Folkestone in the morning. We can easily be on it if we leave early enough tonight."

Auriol lifted her head. Her eyes were dry but they were full of grief. "I need never see him again," she said, almost to herself and a pain shot through her heart like a knife. She shook her head. "No, I cannot go. I cannot condemn you to a life of misery, Crispin. I would have no money. In running away from him I shall relinquish all right to it. 'Twas different before but now he is my husband the law is on his side."

He smiled complacently. "You have enough jewels, do you not?"

She nodded. "Thousands of pounds worth, I think. My emeralds alone . . ."

"He cannot prevent you from taking them with you. They will support us grandly on the continent. Only come with me, my darling, and he will never hurt you again."

He gathered her hands in his and she leaned against him, stiffening suddenly at the sound of a familiar laugh, relaxed and lighthearted as she so rarely heard it. She raised her head and held her breath and a moment later at the end of the walk the Duke was seen to pass by, walking close to a woman who was none other than Madame Gillray. He was looking down on her as they walked slowly together, unaware of being observed. He bent his head to say something in her ear and she laughed gaily at whatever he had said.

Auriol shuddered when they were gone from sight. "What do we do, Auriol?" Crispin whispered. His lips found hers and she clung desperately to him for a moment before drawing away.

"Oh, please take me away, Crispin, I beg of you! Take me away!"

VII

Hannah stared at her mistress as if she had taken leave of her senses as Auriol piled all her jewellery into one box and turned the key.

"But, madam, you cannot just *go*. Where is the Duke? What will he say?"

Auriol, sniffing back her tears, had changed from her rich silk gown into one that was less ostentatious and had bid Hannah to pack a portmanteau which now stood waiting by the door. She glanced quickly round the room in case anything had been forgotten. There was so much that would have to be left behind.

"The Duke," she said in a choked voice, "will not miss me until it is too late, and whatever he says and does then will be to no avail.

"He will not care; he did not even escort me home," she added in injured tones, "but instructed his brother-in-law to do so, whilst he went off with Madame Gillray."

"Oh, ma'am," Hannah answered in awe.

Auriol had removed the concoction of spring flowers she had worn in her hair. "She was wearing plums in her hair. *Plums*, Hannah. And he prefers *her* to *me*."

"I shouldn't have thought you'd care," Hannah murmured but Auriol went on as if she had not heard.

"I left early though, with Mr Dainton. He will be returning soon and I must be ready."

"Oh, ma'am are you sure you are doing the right thing?" Hannah asked, wringing her hands in despair. " 'Twill not be easy to settle in a foreign country."

"I speak the language."

" 'Tis still foreign, ma'am."

Auriol paused to look at her maid in an agony of despair. "I am fully aware of what I am giving up, Hannah, but in truth I am giving up very little, for the full story will be around Town in a matter of days.

"I cannot remain here to public ridicule and scorn, Hannah, and I am most fortunate to have Mr Dainton who will care for me devotedly."

Hannah did not look impressed. "He will get the better of the bargain."

Auriol took one last look around her room. "What does it signify? I shall escape; that is all that matters to me now."

Hannah started towards the door. "I'll fetch my cloak and not keep you waiting."

"No, Hannah!" The girl stopped. "You shall not accompany me this time." Her face relaxed into a smile. "The Duke will not take you back; you have already been warned by him, so you know that. It didn't matter on that other occasion, but you have your own life to lead now. Your future with Bennet to think of. I would want you to know happiness even if I cannot."

Hannah stood erect, her mouth set in a stubborn line. "I certainly have no intention of allowing you to go without me, ma'am. Who, for instance, would dress your hair and press your clothes? I'd not entrust one of those Frenchies to do it. No, if I stayed behind, ma'am, I'd not know another moment's peace for the rest of my life."

Auriol smiled. "Bless you, Hannah. But what about Bennet and your plans for the future?"

"I'll see you safely settled a while and then, perhaps, I shall take my chance with His Grace and return to throw myself on his mercy."

Auriol's face grew hard. "He has none."

"Well," said Hannah philosophically, "it may be just as well if all females suffer as you have done at the hands of a man. And I have not even your rank or fortune."

Auriol had to laugh and while the girl was gone she hugged Suki to her, only putting her into the basket when Hannah returned, dressed for travelling in what seemed a remarkably quick time.

"You take the portmanteau, Hannah," Auriol ordered, "and I shall take the jewel box and Suki's basket."

The maidservant did as she was told and preceded her mistress into the corridor. Auriol paused in the doorway to look behind her but she could see nothing for the tears that blinded her eyes.

VIII

The Duke rested languidly on the couch in Marie Gillray's boudoir. This room, which was once as familiar to him as any in his own homes, now seemed very strange.

As he awaited the lady, he helped himself liberally of grapes from a dish of fruit at his elbow. The air was heavy with the scent of patchouli which made him want to sneeze. Unconsciously it suddenly brought to mind the freshness of his wife's eau de cologne that she always wore but which never seemed too heavy.

When he heard a noise in the doorway he turned his head slightly to see Marie standing there wearing only a gown of the finest tiffany, which hid nothing of the person beneath it.

He caught his breath at the sight of her and she smiled, well aware of her effect on him and gratefully reassured that it had not waned in the interval between their last meeting. She came further into the room and suddenly, as he started to laugh, her look of complacency faded.

"You find me amusing?" she asked stiffly, for this was something she had not expected.

"Not you, Marie, but whatever possessed you to wear *plums* in your hair?"

She stiffened with indignation. "My eyes are violet."

"They are not like plums."

In her dismay her hand went to her elaborately dressed head, but her fingers could not quite touch the height in which the fruit nestled.

"You do not like them?"

"They look ridiculous, but," he added more kindly in the face of her dismay, "the rest of you is magnificent."

Marie Gillray was mollified to some degree and walked about the room in order that he could see and admire her body the better. She had never failed to enchant him before, so she had no reason to believe tonight would be the first time.

"It's that fool of a hairdresser," she said peevishly. "This is the last time he will dress my hair."

"I have always told you that man is a fool, but, now," he said, more briskly, "what is this matter on which you have to see me so urgently?"

She turned to face him and pouted prettily. "I just wanted to see you, of course, *chéri*."

"But what is so urgent about that? I could have called in tomorrow, could I not?"

She stared at him in disbelief. "Dominic, it has been so long."

The Duke drew a sigh. "I am aware of that, my dear, but you must own my duties of late have become decidedly onerous."

"They never were before, *chéri*. Why, I recall one occasion when you left my bed to fight a duel, and, *mon dieu*, you won it!"

The Duke looked vaguely embarrassed at the reminder of his past follies. "I am not so young or so foolish now."

She laughed but there was a forced sound about it, and he began to rise from his seat. "Well, if you have nothing more to impart I must away."

She hurried towards him and flung herself against him. "Oh, no, *chéri*. I have missed you so very much, *mon amour*. Please do not leave me now."

Her exquisite face looked up into his, her lips were moist, inviting him, and he could not resist her. Indeed, he could not understand why he had wanted to. He had not consciously avoided her; he had just not found time to seek her company and until now when she pressed against him and he could feel the outline of her body against his he had not missed her.

But now his arms enfolded her as their lips met. Marie Gillray was triumphant as she sensed the response to her embrace and when she drew away she pulled him down on to the couch beside her.

"Oh, *chéri*, we will not be parted again." She took his face between her hands and he kissed her again. Breathlessly she said, as his lips caressed her neck. "It will be just as it was before; better, oh, much better, my love, as you promised me it would be once you were married and free of all financial restraint."

Suddenly he drew away, staring at her as if she

were a stranger instead of the woman who had, as a mere boy, initiated him into the mysteries of manhood. How long ago that was; when Auriol Stanford was still in the nursery.

Marie Gillray looked perplexed as his eyes raked her, taking note of her still flawless face and the knowing look of a woman confident of her charms, her ripe body which she could so expertly use to entice a man to madness. In that moment he knew conclusively why he had not hastened to his *chère amie* the moment he had come in to Town. As he gazed at this woman who had entranced him for so long, he could see only a pair of green eyes filled with perplexity and of anguish, and of lips which kissed only his.

"I am sorry, Marie, I have not made myself plain. It cannot be as it was before." He got to his feet again and looked down on her, feeling nothing but vague pity for her. "Time marches on and we must change with it, my dear . . ."

Her hand went to her throat just as if someone were squeezing it as she continued to gaze at him in disbelief. "You are drunk. You must be to say such a thing to me."

"I am sober, Marie," he told her in as gentle a voice as he could contrive, for in truth he was desperately anxious to away now.

It was not too late, he knew, to beg Auriol's forgiveness; to begin again, to wipe out all that had occurred since the letter from Crispin Dainton had soured the beginnings of happiness. She could not still love that man, he told himself.

" 'Tis better to end on a pleasant note." he told Marie Gillray, almost unthinkingly as he thought of his wife who would be awaiting him at home. This very night he would be with her again, for it was she whom he desired above all others. "You will not be lonely for too long, I think."

To his surprise her eyes filled with tears. "You have found someone else. Only tell me who she is, for I cannot conceive who it can be. No word of it has come to my ears . . ."

He smiled. "You will not credit this, Marie, and you will think me addle-brained but I have an unfashionable fondness for the woman I married."

He drew a deep sigh of satisfaction at having admitted it at last. In some way it was like seeing the sky and the sun after years of imprisonment in a dark dungeon.

"Goodbye, Marie," he said as he made towards the door. "I have many happy memories of you, which I shall always cherish, as I hope you have of me."

As he turned to go she sprang to her feet. "You liar! It cannot be your wife. You hate her. You as much as told me so on the night you married her. I was puzzled then but I know why now, so you cannot be fond of *her*! 'Tis impossible."

He swung round on his heel. His benign expression was no more. He came back towards her, his eyes flashing with fury.

"What do you know?"

Marie Gillray bit her lip and began to back away from him. She shook her head. "About her father cheating yours, that is all I know."

"Where did you hear that, Marie?"

"Your sister—Lady D'Ouro—told me."

He smiled grimly. "Don't gammon me, Marie. Madelaine would never tell *you*."

She had backed up against the wall and could go no further. He stood in front of her and she managed a weak smile. The realisation that she could no longer make him do anything she wished had thrown her into a blind panic. This was a man she did not know how to handle and it was the first time she had suffered the experience.

"She did not consciously do so, Dominic. She believed I already knew of it, and I did not enlighten her."

"You will not speak of it again to anyone in any circumstances, Marie," he told her in a quiet voice that was nonetheless resolute, and she nodded her eager agreement.

"No, indeed I will not, but you must come back to me. You must, Dominic."

"Not if you were the only woman left alive in the world."

He began to walk away from her and she cried in desperation, heedless of his anger now, "She will not be there!"

He paused again and Marie Gillray said, breathlessly triumphant now, "You may not want me, Dominic, but she does not want you. Is that not ironic?" She laughed and there was an edge of hysteria to it.

"I told Crispin Dainton about your reasons for marrying her and he has persuaded her to run away with him. You will not catch them now."

His face twisted into a grimace of fury and she was afraid again. She attempted to run to her bedroom but he caught her, clamping his hand around her neck.

"You have contrived this, you whore! I could kill you."

He shook her as easily as if she were a rag doll and even though she struggled to free herself she could not manage it. She saw murder in his eyes then and was more afraid than ever before.

At last he released her and she fell back, nursing her bruised throat.

"Where are they bound?" he snapped.

"I don't know," she answered in a hoarse voice.

He seized her again by the neck and squeezed so hard that she had to fight for breath. Her nails raked his hand but he did not relinquish his hold on her. His anger and despair gave him added strength.

"I vow I will kill you if you do not tell me."

When he released her again she could not speak for a few moments, and then she croaked, "To Folkestone to catch the morning packet to France."

He stepped back a pace. "Have you mentioned this story to anyone else apart from Dainton?" She shook her head. "If ever, Marie, you mention this matter to anyone again I shall ensure that no man will ever bear to look at you again."

She began to cry and it was the first time during their long association that he had seen her do so.

"I did it so that we could be together as you wished so often, and now you behave in this heartless way towards one who has loved you all these years."

"You don't know what love is and you are deserving of my bad treatment, which is more than I can say of the sweet girl who married me against her will and then tried to make the best of it."

He walked away from her in disgust. "I could have

had such fond memories of you, Marie. Now, because I may have lost her for ever because of you, I despise you."

She was sobbing hysterically now. "You loved me," she wailed, and his heart despite all was stirred to pity. "You said you would always love me."

"I did not know what love is, Marie," he said softly. "I knew only how to hate."

Tears streamed down her face as she watched him go from her for the last time; still dazed with disbelief, for it was inconceivable that her carefully laid plans should have gone so disastrously awry.

"Dominic," she called to him in anguish, but he had already gone.

Sobbing even more wildly she stumbled into her bedroom, sending a chair which was in her way crashing to the floor. Maddened even more now she called for Hélène as she sank down before her mirror, and then she caught sight of her ravaged face which now looked so old, and in anger she began to hit out at everything near to hand. Her wig stand went crashing to the floor and then a porcelain powder bowl, her patch box and a tray of rouges.

Not content with the destruction she had already caused she threw a candlestick at the mirror which cracked from top to bottom, splintering like a spider's web and blotted out the image of herself that she hated.

"Hélène!" she cried again. "Have you deserted me too?"

It was then the abigail appeared. She came running into her mistress's room and stopped wide-eyed in the doorway at the sight of such destruction and her hysterical mistress.

"*Le diable!*" she cried. "What has happened here?"

At the appearance of her maid Marie Gillray stopped her rampaging. The fury died out of her and she said piteously, "He has left me, Hélène!"

And with a sigh she crumpled into unconsciousness on the floor.

IX

From the window of her private parlour in "The Ancient Mariner" Inn, Auriol could see ships at anchor in the harbour. She was sitting back against the window seat, staring out at the scene which in other circumstances would have charmed her. But today her eyes pricked with fatigue, for she had slept little. The carriage hired by Mr Dainton had not been a comfortable one and even if it had been of the best, the roads were so bad that a jolting was unavoidable when they travelled at such speed.

The sea stretched unendingly from the harbour. Soon, she knew, she would be crossing that stretch of water to a strange land and a new life.

Suki jumped up on to the window seat to be beside her, glad of the freedom from her travelling basket, and Auriol stroked her pet fondly.

She would never see the Duke again, she told herself, and therefore should be overjoyed. She was going to be with the man she truly loved, but her mind kept recalling a time at Hampden Towers when happiness with the Duke had not seemed so far away. Auriol would not admit to being emotional at the thought of not being able to melt so hard a heart, for she was determined that she had never wanted to, but nevertheless she buried her face in Suki's fur so she need not blink back her tears.

The door opened and she looked up sharply, forcing a smile to her lips when she saw Crispin. She was determined not to let her sadness be apparent to the one who was doing so much to help her.

He came quickly across the room and sat down on the window seat facing her. "I have secured a passage for us on the packet," he told her delightedly. "We leave in an hour."

"How wonderful," she said in a choked voice. "All is going according to plan."

He glanced around the room and his eyes came to rest on the cold collation which still remained untouched on the table. He looked at her in dismay then.

"You have not eaten at all, Auriol."

She smiled at him reassuringly. "I am not hungry. All I want is sleep, Crispin, and that I shall have in plenty on the boat. The sea appears to be calm today."

"It is a fine day for a voyage, I am told by the old salts down by the harbour. You may sleep the entire voyage away," he told her, his voice softening, "And when you awake it will be to a new life—with me."

He raised her chin so that he could look at her face.

"Once we are away from England and from him those dark shadows around your eyes will fade, my love."

He drew her closer and was about to kiss her when Suki growled deep in her throat and jumped between them on the window seat.

Crispin Dainton sat back immediately, looking vexed. "I wonder you had to bring that wretched beast with you, Auriol. You know he dislikes me."

Auriol looked hurt and held Suki even closer. "I could go nowhere without Suki. Even the Duke would not have wished me to do so."

"Pah! The Duke," he said in disgust. "You may forget all about him my dear, for you are lost to him now. He will be at this very moment asleep in the arms of his mistress. She is a woman who will suit him far better than you. They are both unscrupulous people."

"Aren't we all when we search for happiness?" she mused.

He stood up and stretched his spine. "Ah, I do declare it will be good not to have to elude the duns any more."

She looked at him sharply. "You are in debt, Crispin?"

He looked sheepish then. "Only a few small bills, my dear. I shall settle them all in due course, never you fear." He walked across to the table and surveyed the food. "The good sea air has given me an appetite. Are you sure you will not join me?"

He glanced at her and she shook her head, after which he started to pile his plate with an assortment of meats.

He paused momentarily to gaze into space. "I think

we shall take a house in Paris for a while," he mused. "Do you not fancy the idea?"

He awaited her answer, which she gave with a watery smile, "Whatever you decide, Crispin. I hardly think it matters where we are. The Duke will divorce me with no blame attached to him, and possessed of my fortune will be free to marry his . . . Madame Gillray."

"We can then marry if you wish it, my dear." He came back to the window seat with his plate. "We can travel in Italy later. You will like that I am certain. The world is ours, my love. There is nowhere we cannot go."

"Except England." Auriol sighed, envying him the appetite that allowed him to consume his meal so heartily.

They sat in silence whilst he ate and then when he had finished he sighed with satisfaction, taking out his watch. "Not much longer, my dear. I hope that abigail of yours is not going to be late."

"She is only securing some small items I forgot to bring with me," she told him, wondering if future conversations with Crispin would ever be as stimulating as those she had had with the Duke.

It is my marriage I am running away from, she reminded herself, and then angrily told herself; it was no marriage.

He took his plate back to the table and as he put it down there came the sound of raised voices outside. Auriol and Crispin looked at each other in surprise and wonder but before either of them could voice a question or investigate the commotion the parlour door burst open and the Duke stood framed in the doorway.

Auriol shrank back automatically as her eyes met his. He was beside himself with rage; only one glance at him told her that. She looked towards the other man who stood as if turned to stone. The colour had completely drained from his face. To Auriol it was like reliving a particularly horrific nightmare.

There was a full minute of stunned silence and then incongruously Suki jumped down from Auriol's lap and flew across the room barking with joy. Her action broke the tension and, distracted for the moment, the Duke looked down on her and his expression softened, but it was gone in a second.

His eyes found Auriol's face again. "Dammit, Madam, call this pup off."

"Come here this instant, Suki!" she called, and the animal did so, although she continued to pant and to wag her tail at the Duke who slammed the door closed, shutting out several pairs of curious eyes.

"So," he said, addressing Crispin through his teeth, "you have seen fit to interfere in my family affairs for the second time." His hand went to the hilt of his sword. "I vow you will not do so a third time. Prepare to defend yourself."

Auriol ran to him, blocking the way to Crispin. Suki, unaware of the drama, frisked at their heels.

"Don't I beg of you, Your Grace. I will do anything you ask of me to avoid bloodshed."

He held her gaze for a moment or two as she pleaded so eloquently with her eyes, but it was Crispin who said, "Stand aside, Auriol. This matter must be settled here and now."

He drew his sword and Auriol saw the anger spark in her husband's eyes again. "Insolent puppy!" he roared. "Who gave you leave to address my wife in such familiar tones?"

He pushed Auriol to one side, saying as he stared furiously at his opponent, "Leave the room, Duchess. I would not have you see him cut to ribbons by my sword."

"You have yet to do it, Duke," Crispin retorted, and Auriol stamped her foot on the floor.

"Stop this foolishness! I demand that you cease such childishness."

But she might as well have saved herself the effort of speaking. The Duke pushed her further into the corner, saying, "Do not move from there, Duchess."

"Oh, *please*," she said in one last appeal as their swords met and clashed.

She stooped down quickly to pick up the excited spaniel and held her close in her arms. The parlour was not a large one and as the men fought grimly pieces of furniture crashed to the floor and were sent spinning into a corner. Outside the room a buzz of excitement went up as a crowd gathered to see the outcome.

The Duke was a renowned swordsman and after a minute or two Auriol was relieved to see that Crispin had improved his arm and was holding his own. The slaughter of the younger man she had so clearly envisaged had not yet occurred. She closed her eyes for she could not watch the fight, but she could not close her ears to the steady clash of steel around the room.

Suddenly Suki yelped as if hurt and Auriol opened her eyes to see that the Duke had smashed the sword from Crispin's hand. It clattered to the ground and the young man had his back against the wall. His eyes were filled with fear. Auriol cried out in alarm and Suki, with another yelp, jumped out of her arms and flew across the room. The Duke, caught unawares, glanced behind him, tripped over Suki's little body and went crashing to the floor.

A look of triumph flashed across Crispin Dainton's face. He snatched up his fallen sword and made to plunge it into the breast of the man who now lay helpless at his feet. Auriol saw what was about to happen in a flash. She darted forward, crying, "Don't kill him!" but with such unexpected victory in his grasp Crispin Dainton did not even hear her. He lunged forward with his sword.

"No!" she screamed, throwing herself on top of the Duke, screaming again as the cold steel thrust into her side plunging her into oblivion.

For a moment there was a shocked silence in the room as Crispin Dainton stared in disbelief at what he had done. Slowly he withdrew the point of his sword as the Duke gently raised himself, cradling Auriol in his arms as he did so. One arm went round her waist as he sought to find her wound with his free hand. Blood began to seep through the thin stuff of her gown and he looked at his hand as it came away from the wound covered in blood.

He kept on staring at his hand as if he had never seen it before and so did the other man. Then the Duke looked up at him, his face twisting in anger and in despair as he cried, "You've killed her! Damn you in hell; you've killed her!"

X

The physician stood back from the modest bed in what was the best chamber "The Ancient Mariner" had to offer. He watched the pale figure beneath the sheets for a few moments and then looked across to the Duke who waited at the end of the bed.

"Well, Doctor?" he asked impatiently when the man did not speak.

The doctor merely shook his head. Hannah began to sniff into her handkerchief as the Duke drew the physician, none too gently, into the corner of the room.

"Why do you shake your head so?" he asked breathlessly, "Have you no tongue in your head with which to speak?"

"There is nothing left that I can do to help Her

215

Grace," the physician said gravely. "I have done all I can; she is beyond any human help now."

"Be plain," said the Duke through his teeth, for he was sorely tempted to shake this bungling clod until his marble teeth rattled in his skull.

The physician sighed. "The Duchess is dying, Your Grace."

"Dying." The word came out as a sigh. He glanced towards the bed, looking upon his wife's face, bloodless and as pale almost as the pillow itself. And then he looked to the physician again. "You cannot allow her to *die*. You are a doctor, are you not?"

He did shake the man now, roughly too. "I am a physician, Your Grace, not a magician. The case, I own, is a puzzling one. Her Grace was not mortally wounded, for the sword did not damage any organ, nor is there poisoning . . ."

"Then why, man?"

The doctor drew himself up with dignity and straightened his wig which the Duke's shaking had dislodged. "I do not know. There is no reason why she should not recover, wounded as she is, but Her Grace does not seem to want to recover. She is making no effort to fight for her own life; that is the essence of it."

The Duke drew back as if stung. "I will not allow her to die," he said fiercely. "It is I who should have received that sword thrust. She tried to save *me*."

"Be that as it may, Your Grace, there is nothing more I can do."

The Duke eyed him belligerently and the physician knew fear, for the Duke's ways were well known. "I was told you were the best available."

The man bowed at the compliment and the Duke went on, fingering his purse. "I shall pay anything to save her," he promised. "Whatever you ask shall be yours. Name your price."

The physician smiled faintly. "Not for the crown jewels can I do more for her." He put on his hat. "I shall call again on the morrow, if she still lives."

"If . . ." echoed the Duke explosively.

He dashed over to the bed, pushing aside the weeping abigail and seizing hold of Auriol by the shoulders.

"Your Grace . . ." the physician complained, but he spoke in vain.

"Duchess," the Duke said angrily to his unconscious wife, "you will not die. Dammit, woman, do you hear me? You will obey me for once. I will not let you die!"

"She cannot hear you," the physician told him, "so do not distress yourself, Your Grace. It is God's will."

"It cannot be God's will that she die for me!"

The Duke gazed down in disbelief at his wife's face; incredibly she was even more beautiful in repose. Her eyes were closed but he remembered how fiery they were when they flashed with anger—with life— greener than the most brilliant of emeralds. There was no colour in her lips either, but he could easily recall how red they were without the aid of rouge, how moist and inviting, and guileless and innocent. How he had abused them.

He looked up unseeingly at the physician. "No," he said harshly. "No, I won't let her leave me now."

He gathered the inert form into his arms. So slight

was she, she might have been a child. He cradled her to him gently now, his shoulder supporting her head.

"Don't leave me, Duchess," he said softly. "Don't leave me in misery, for if you do I shall die too."

XI

Auriol opened her eyes slowly. She felt as though she were the princess in the fairy tale and had been asleep for a hundred years. The first person she saw was her mother, who had been sitting at the side of the bed since the hasty summons and the Duke's carriage had arrived.

"Mama," Auriol whispered and she was answered by the relief in her mother's smile. She got to her feet quickly to lean over the bed so that Auriol need not raise her voice to be heard.

"Mama, I dreamed Dominic was here."

"And so I am," he said coming into her line of vision.

At that moment she was not to know how thin and haggard she, herself, appeared so she derived a shock from the sight of him so hollow eyed. He still wore his bloodstained breeches, but no coat, and his shirt was soiled too. His face looked as if it had not been shaved for days and he was so far removed from the immaculately attired and groomed man she had seen before.

She put one hand out towards him, which he took in his and raised to his lips. "It was not a dream," she breathed.

Somewhere near a door closed behind Mrs Ardmore who thought it fitting to leave the room at that point.

She kept on looking at him in wonder. There was nothing either of them could find to say in those first few precious moments of discovery. The moment was shattered then by Suki who jumped on to the bed. Auriol was too weak to take her but the sight of her pet reminded her of the duel.

"Suki," she gasped weakly. " 'Tis all your fault." The spaniel climbed down again, her tail between her legs. "She tripped you, Dominic."

"She knew no better, but what is my excuse?" he asked in a sober voice.

She turned her face into the pillow and at that moment a sharp pain stabbed at her and she gasped. The soft look upon his face gave way to one of concern.

"You are in pain!"

The pain went as suddenly as it came and she smiled.

"It has gone. There is no pain any more."

He sank down on to the edge of the bed, his head bent over her hand. "I have caused you so much of it, Duchess. Can you forgive me and allow me a chance to make you happy?"

"There is nothing to forgive, Dominic. You are

willing to forget everything and that is all that matters."

"I shall never forget that you almost died to save me."

She withdrew her hand. "Is that why . . . ?"

"No," he breathed, feasting his eyes on her face again. "I love you. I just cannot live without you, Duchess. You are what makes my life worth living and without you I may as well be dead."

Tears welled up in her eyes, her eyelashes sparkled with tiny tear drops and she gave a contented smile.

Then she opened her eyes wide in alarm. "Mr Dainton. What has happened to him?"

The Duke's facial muscles tightened. "He escaped me in the concern for you. I believe he is now in France. He will not dare to return, I fancy. Do you . . ." he asked hesitantly, "care?"

"I care only for you, Dominic. Only I could no longer bear you to hate me so and when I learned it was common knowledge about my father I knew I must go. I could not face the scandal of everyone knowing why you married me."

The Duke looked away. "Have no fear, there will be no talk. Only Madame Gillray, aside from Mr Dainton, knows the story—which I did not tell her—and Marie will not tell." She watched him carefully, knowing he was finding it difficult to talk. "It was Marie who encouraged Dainton to elope with you and when I discovered it I told her my real feelings for her . . . and for you. She . . . I am told . . . had a seizure after I left, for which I truly pity her. There is little hope for her recovery although she may linger on as an invalid for years."

"Oh, Dominic, the poor woman."

"Do not pity her, Duchess. She almost caused your death, as I did with my wicked schemes, and yet it is I, the most guilty of all, who is escaping retribution. In possessing your love I am actually being rewarded for my sins."

"Oh no," she said softly. "I am not an easy person to live with, Dominic, as you have already discovered. There will be many a disagreement ahead of us yet."

He smiled. "I certainly hope so, Duchess."

"You may yet live to regret marrying me."

"Never," he vowed, taking her hand in his once more.

He smoothed back her tangle of hair and she said, "I'll wager I look a wreck just now."

"You have never looked more beautiful, my love.

"And now you must sleep and recover your strength. I order you to." She closed her eyes and her eyelashes fanned out on her cheeks. The Duke drew a sigh, swallowed a lump in his throat and said a silent prayer of thanks before saying, "When you are well enough, Duchess, we shall go to Hampden Towers. You will soon grow strong again there."

"I should love that above all things, Dominic," she answered without opening her eyes. "We were almost happy there."

"We will be happy there. Happier than any couple who ever lived. Now you must rest or we shall have to remain here for weeks and I shall be forced to endure more nights on that infernal truckle bed they set up for me."

She chuckled. "I am so tired 'tis amazing. But stay here with me while I sleep. I shall know it if you do."

"I wouldn't want to be anywhere else."

Suki, determined not to be left out of anything, came running to his feet and sat looking at them both, hand in hand, thumping her tail on the floor in approval.

FAWCETT CREST
BESTSELLERS